FOURTEEN STORIES, NONE OF THEM ARE YOURS

a novel

Praise for *Fourteen Stories, None of Them Are Yours*

"About twenty pages into Luke B. Goebel's *Fourteen Stories, None of Them Are Yours,* I realized I was reading with one hand holding my forehead and one balled at my waist, kind of clenched and gazing down into the paper, like a man soon to be converged upon. Goebel's testimony comes on like that: engrossing, fanatical, full of private grief, and yet, at the same time, charismatic, tender, and intrepid, aglow with more spirit than most Americans have the right to wield."

—**Blake Butler**, author of *Nothing* and *Scorch Atlas*

"I'm in love with language again, because Luke B. Goebel is not afraid to take us back through the gullet of loss into the chaos of words. Someone burns a manuscript in Texas; someone's speed sets a life on fire; a heart is beaten nearly to death, the road itself is the trip, a man is decreated back to his animal past—better, beyond ego, beautiful, and look: there's an American dreamscape left. There's a reason to go on."

—**Lidia Yuknavitch**, author of *Liberty's Excess* and *Dora: A Headcase*

"Luke may be one of the last few geniuses we have left in this life. I mean that. He's a good boy with a lot of pain in his heart."

—**Scott McClanahan**, author of *Crapalachia* and *Hill William*

"The protagonist of *Fourteen Stories, None of Them Are Yours* doesn't make it easy for us, channeling as he does Barry Hannah and Denis Johnson by way of Rick Bass and Dennis Hopper, and self-presenting as yet another damaged romantic who thinks it's always time to play the cowboy, skating in and out of sense. He can't see right, and he's haunted by nearly everything. He's trying to open up or shut himself down or at least get a hold of himself. He's trying to make do with what he's done, while he reminds us that we're all, one way or another, in that position."

—**Jim Shepard**, National Book Award finalist and author of the short story collections *You Think That's Bad* and *Like You'd Understand, Anyway*

FOURTEEN STORIES, NONE OF THEM ARE YOURS

a novel

LUKE B. GOEBEL

TUSCALOOSA

The University of Alabama Press
Tuscaloosa, Alabama 35487-0380

Manufactured in the United States of America

FC2 is an imprint of The University of Alabama Press

Book Design: Illinois State University's English Department's Publications Unit; Codirectors: Steve Halle and Jane L. Carman; Assistant Director: Danielle Duvick; Production Assistant: Taylor Birch
Cover Design: Lou Robinson
Typeface: Garamond
Acknowledgments: "Insides" appeared in *Elimae*; "The Adventures of Eagle Feather" appeared in *New York Tyrant* "Boot of the Boot" appeared in *Unsaid*; "Before Carl Left" appeared in *Wigleaf*; "Tough Beauty" appeared in *The American Reader*; "Apache" appeared in *Green Mountains Review*; "Hogs" appeared in *Everyday Genius* under the penname Bridger Redmond; "Out There" appeared in *[PANK]*; "America, America, America" appeared in *Trnsfr*. Text and titles have in certain cases been altered since the original publication.

∞

The paper on which this book is printed meets the minimum requirements of American National Standard for Information Sciences—Permanence of Paper for Printed Library Materials, ANSI Z39.48–1984

Library of Congress Cataloging-in-Publication Data
Goebel, Luke B., 1980-
Fourteen stories : none of them are yours : a novel / Luke B. Goebel.
pages cm
ISBN 978-1-57366-180-5 (pbk. : alk. paper) -- ISBN 978-1-57366-847-7 (ebook)
1. Psychic trauma--Fiction. 2. Recreational vehicles--Fiction. I. Title.
PS3607.O333F77 2014
813'.6--dc23

2014005183

This book is dedicated to my big and
only brother—he rode on ahead—Carl.

For our sister, Marie.

CONTENTS

FOURTEEN STORIES, NONE OF THEM ARE YOURS

a novel

INSIDES

IN THE HOSPITAL. In the gown. On the gurney. Strange me but I love it here. I like the inside. I'd rather be well, but I love to hear the people speak. An old woman in her room wants to speak sputum. I hear garbage bags being opened. I'm on a hospital bed not a gurney. I hear crinkling sounds. The rush and flock of life's little hospital-bound disasters. Even in my little room. I can't believe I get to be in the world. I have always felt like I'm getting away with something being alive. Even though it's the usual cases of shit—nervous breakdowns on peyote, cowering in my mind, getting myself back together with it, moving from hotel to hospital to behind the wheel.

How about a JOKE: A man, let's call him Harry. Harry goes into an interview in old New York City. There is a great big man behind the desk, an outdoorsman-looking man, even in his finery and top office. You can tell he is an outdoorsman, among other things, by the occasional artifact placed here or there, the pictures on his desk of his duck-hunting dog, by the duck-hunting dog itself, Buck, lying on his carpeted floor. Let's say the interview starts and Harry has terrible gas. He is trying to hold it. He's a young guy looking for a first real gig in the city. He has some good connections and a highfalutin education. He answers the first question fine but out comes Harry flatulating. Luckily, Harry thinks, Buck is nearby. He pins it off on the dog. Pretends nothing has happened. Looks at Buck briefly. Pretends to be polite about the indiscretion. Pretends he's hardly even noticed, he's such a guy, Harry is. Well, you know jokes. Every step of the interview, bwaaaarp, another fart from young nervous Harry. "What can you do for me," the old man barks, followed by a further line of questioning. "Qualifications?" "Fwaaart." The old man looks at Harry, Harry looks at Buck, disapprovingly. The interview is going great, Harry decides, as the old man thinks it's Buck. Pretty soon, Harry is sure he has it in the bag! He's bagged the buck by luck by Buck's being there in the room. What luck the old man had a dog! Right then, Harry can't hold it in anymore. He lets one go. "Buck, Buck," the old man shouts. "Bucky, B U C K! Get the hell away from that guy before he shits all over you," the old man says.

I am to have a CTscan.

See, I came to the hospital. No one or me knew what went wrong. Rib pain, lung pain, stomach pain, pain in the guts and groin. Groaning pain doubled me over.

See, I start to hate the old woman in the unseen room. I yell for her to quiet down. She gets sandwiches, I hear, which I don't get any of. She talks of *Anus Parade Nursing Home.* I miss so many words. I get others wrong. I have a life of taking trips with my little mind, all freaked over from long ago and still traveling from the ground out of my head, moving my body around like a Cracker Jack.

I can partly see a sign outside that woman's door. Can't make out the words or pictures. A doctor comes and wears a front plastic coating, gloves, eye gear.

He enters her.

I pick apart a newspaper in my gown. I find the inside pages with pictures of steak, potatoes, Mr. Clean.

We had an IGA we had called Wagner's in Ohio. That's where I grew up: Ohio. It was all pick-up trucks and football, basketball, baseball, then football again. My brother was there, older than I. My sister came next after me. Our church everyone went inside, sun or rain. All the seasons. We had crazy parents who were kids themselves, insane, sweating, shouting and watching everything in sight—Dad had a Connecticut Crusher hat in the hall closet which the hall had a beautiful cold stone floor made of different shaped real tiles cemented together and cobbled. He had suits and long herringbone coats. He had shoes in there. Hat and ties. Things in the coat pockets. Mints and money. He had a job at a fortune 500 company in the Midwest. He had our diesel Mercedes with the leather and the diamond patterns in the leather and all that road all over the place. He had cigs on the way to take us to school far away from where we lived, him gagging and spitting out the window, and crazed, dressed like a pro. Montessori was the school, and our mother found it for us—our mother who tried and tried, fought and hoarded the family money dressed in men's clothes. We had the '80s in America, America, America and the whole trip of being a self within a family within a nation of movies, vacuum cleaners, the whole nine yachts—Reagan, Dennis

Hopper, real records on the wheel in a house, the house we bought from family within our family, with the wood stove with their last name's initial emblazed in gold, movies and no war, just politics, president wearing makeup, hardly any places to raise a chicken or grow a vegetable where most people were going and us with cornfields in the backyard, the little Ohio woods, still plenty of room for chickens and veggies, but also cold weather and the need to go to work for more money in the bank.

Who am I, now, but a weird patient part of all this world, in a little room with a sign about pain? It ranks pain from No Pain, to 1,2,3—Mild Pain, 4,5,6—Moderate Pain, 7,8,9—Severe Pain with faces that show increased crucifixion. 10 is Worst Possible and the face looks about right for the living. I can take the body's betrayal, at first, I think, but I think of Catherine and I'm done for, nearly.

I told her, when she left me, over the telephone, that I had memorized her feet, I told her. I had them sunk in my mind, I told her. I had lust on all over for them, I told her. She waited on me to prove it. She was always waiting on Yours Truly to win her, or I misunderstood. The first times we were together I sucked her feet whole. I licked her from crack to crack. I sat back on her couch, and she stood on the arm and the back of the sofa and lowered herself down to my taste. This was on a terrific street up above a China person's restaurant in NYC. I always feel like a little guy trying to prove I can. She is beyond immaculate. Then I went nuts along her. Mouthed everything.

A nurse puts the ink into me.

Do you know how nervous she makes me? They are going to look inside. Look inside of me. They are going to look inside. I prefer not to think about what's inside. Other than the heart, gut, words. You want to look? Hey, don't look! Hey, hey, don't look in there.

A stroke person is coming from below—being rolled around the halls.

I feel the ink. It is for the CTscan. It is warmer than my blood. It is like a whiskey, hot bourbon, in my lungs and stomach first without throat and I feel I've wet myself and am weak. I feel the warm ink reach my toes. Whiskey is a taste I haven't had since the snow coming sideways through Montana, blinding out the black mountain, long ago with a woman who worked the casinos and cooked beans for me. I'm a living thing in a hospital on my back.

Catherine is from Colorado.

I am from Ohio. Who wins, you figure? Aspen to New York? Or Ohio to hospital?

While inside the CTscan, Oh, I see Jesus Christ. I see serpents. I see lots of things with my eyes shut. Leftovers from mouthfuls of peyote. I wore a blanket around a bunch of Injuns for sixteen hours, plus. Up in Mendocino. Afterwards, we ate ribs out of Styrofoam, store-bought fried chickens, brownies, and Faygo Soda—I looked at the ice of vision on everything in the new day's sun moving—I still don't see like a person.

Now I know I'm not just going to die from suffering. That's what peyote is good for.

Catherine, I don't know?

For the past week I had broken ribs or lung and bone cancer. I went from doctor to doctor holding my side. Tied a dress shirt around my ribs to sleep right at night. The Docs said, "Muscular skeletal, from coughing, those ciggies, hold, it will heal." Bastards! I had only thoughts of Catherine and feeling the hurt side.

I'm Six Foot Five, Six, Seven, and have had pain.

A femur in half, my skull broke a few times, busted arms, some dog bites, cuts and minor burns, distemper, hyper this and that. Mentally unhealthy: family history of alcoholism, drugs, and whatnot.

My grandfather, his father was a banker who owned a bank. His father's father started the bank, made uniforms for the Union army, built engines for coal mining trains. All of them are severe or wild and entrepreneuring in black and white photos in suits. My grandfather started one of his legs on fire thirty-however-many years ago. He burned the eyelets of his boots black into the skin, green hickory fire lit with gasoline, gasoline, leg, Ohio. The old backyard. My origins. He made himself a roastbeef sandwich before he drove up to the hospital. Little horseradish, mustard, on pumpernickel. "They never feed you in those places," he said to his wife, my Mamma. His leg was smelling up the kitchen, the way she tells it—80 years old and clean—them still together humping across the weather. Those two my champion winners, keeping me upright and my family in order, mostly.

So, I waited out pain on a bare futon mattress on my floor at home until here. None of us have the same homes. We are all just looking around a lot of the time. Unless you count some of the great jumping beans I have known. Guys who grunt and hump and hope their way through life. All of them having done time in the nut house bin or prison before. All drugged up and half-drunk. I only did ever jail. I spent my early twenties in rehabs—got used to the music of shifts.

See, I adjusted to the pain, used Icy Hot, had pills and ciggies. Finally, it was thinking of Catherine did me in, and I decided to come to the ER for a jot of R&R. Catherine is in New York City. She says she needs to get herself figured out first. She says she needs to clean house first. She says all sorts of things. Bottom line, I'm suffering from love lost. I've waited till I was about thirty to do more than have sex.

I told her about her feet I'd memorized.

"Your first two toes peek from those red mules," I proved on a phone line to her. I was hunching over standing in my living room with no furniture, side in the kind of pain as one who has been stabbed. "Your bigtoe toenails are symmetrical, rising from their sides to a higher curve of middle," I said.

We had been all throughout New York City. Lived there together. Looked at fine things and plays and walked through talking—never got real sleep. I love how the pigeons will bank crazy with their wings spread high through the angles of a shadow on a summer day in Hell's Kitchen. A dollar slice. The bandaged smells of the subways that are all hers. I was smoking a cig in my living room in the woods. "Your second toes are long," I said, "but not longer. Your other three are nearly the same length as one another. You have high strong arches. Nice little heels. I want to suck on them Baby. Sex, Kitten." She didn't say a word or even giggle. I miss driving when I was fifteen years ago. When I was a jumping jack and didn't think but new pussy and highway. A clot of sun. The sky forever. A song. I hear the old woman coughing her sputum. Steak, potato, then a doctor comes in with no hair.

"Mr. Clean," I address him.

I ask him about the woman. Say I've had it with her. Say I'm not right.

He tells me she's paralyzed from the neck down. Gives me the look like he understands where I am coming from. I cannot remember where I'm coming from. I've been East a long time. I fell in love for the first time with a New York woman. I haven't had any steak. I think it'd be Christian to put that old woman out of this life.

Lately, I've been keeping lakeside in my cottage in western New York. I teach freshman college. The other day, middle of class, me showing them all who's boss, a woman's voice is climbing through the scales. She's singing up my spine. I got tears in my face. The kids are all staring at me. Sometimes it's unbreakable how the beauty of art comes after you, making you feel everything and bawl in front of the very people you're supposed to be hectoring. I felt every moment of her singing after she was finished, singing up through my spine. I had to walk home and leave everyone behind.

You know why we get sick?

Giving away what we should have kept.

A few days ago, before I came here, a fox showed while I was on the floor. It looked sick. He was on my porch and I am lying in the room on the floormat playing with myself naked to the fall, the whole great long stretch of my body. Since peyote animals come to me. I was playing with myself to shoots of orange like bayonets on majestic New York trees. The sliding door open to all the colors. I can almost get quiet, nearly, at times. Sometimes the sky opens in light through a window.

This is, it seems, all of any God, until moments when God comes near.

The little tail was thin and wispy, the eyes nearly closed, it wobbled from side to side. I was jerking off trying not to hurt the ribs. I'd been thinking of Catherine's big nipples, her Greek pussy, her big ass and tiny middle. Her green eyes her dark hair and pale skin with blue veins. She has golden circuits around each pupil. She rode on a motor scooter in the rain with me through Spain on a vast freeway. There is nothing outside of America. Semitrailers whizzing by. Love is when you start watching dirty movies and wind up thinking of someone you've had your penis in and wind up turning off the movie. Let me rephrase that: I had started a dirty movie and thought of Catherine and turned it off and thought more of her.

Once my father and me and my brother went to Montana. When Brother was a few years old, Carl, he had spinal meningitis. He snapped out of it. All that was left over was a twitch and a squeak. First cast, a trout through the eye, my brother! He was always so calmly brown eyed and beautiful. When I was a few years older than 7 or so, I broke my arm badly in several places. I was so impressed with the hospital, with the doctors, rooms, all the people, the fluorescents and smells, the difference between being inside and outside of a place, I forgot all about the arm. See, Doc starts telling me jokes and chatting up my mother, a real looker and rich, sets the arm, pulls the cast on the other. It takes hours to get home, and I realize the mistake—sometimes it's like that when I think of Catherine. Sometimes I wish I had more jokes.

I made another mistake and dated my first girlfriend. This was at eighteen. I thought I was a man and wore a woman's fur coat around with my hair long. A huge black negroid tried to hold me up for cash outside of the club where she worked. She worked taking off her clothes like a boy. That's how she looked on stage. Hey, it's work! I don't judge. Look, I told that man, *flatten me*. He was six-foot-ten and full of jails and sperm.

He started laughing and gripped crotch. He shot his head toward me. Giant. He could have murdered me in one shot. I was impressed. He wound cloth around his knuckles. I couldn't wait for the jets overhead to knock me back. But he just starts laughing and shaking his head at me, and gets into his car and asks me and my girl, who'd come out and started smoking and yelling at *me*, if we needed to get to someplace. She had just come out the club's exit. Me and her crawled in. It was a great old Cadillac coach with a leather roof, but the interior was shot to pilling and ratty fabric, the foam busting through armrests. She was the kind of little girl who had a dildo that plugged into the wall and it had a long cord and the end she put inside her was a terrible color of skin. I hate that I tell everything, but it's all I got to work with.

After I saw her use it, and her paintings, I didn't really want to touch her or watch her dance, but we were together.

She and that man decided to make it. It was my fault. I had to walk all the way back home and eventually to my kin.

When I was 19 it was jail plus rehabs. When I was 20, it was rehab plus rehab. When I was 21, rehab again two more times. I am not a dainty soul when drunk and never wanted not to be not blacked out. This was the last time, at 21, but the night guards made such a nice sound walking around at night guarding us. I wish I could go back! Life was simpler. Here I am. Here you are too.

There was an Armenian man doing one rehab with me. Harry. He would tell me sometimes he couldn't get it up, but Harry's tongue always worked overtime, he said. He looked at me so blankly with trouble behind the blanks. He was enormous and showed me his tongue. It was full of bumps. That's all they want, he told me.

I've tried that approach myself, when I first started seeing Catherine. On account of I could not get functioning. That's how much I was in love. We met in our teacher's class, a wildly famous man with feathers and grease cloth for clothing in NYC. A real genius California Indian Gun Nut from NY. It took time to get over that and get it worked out. Me and her. Him and her.

There was another guy, he had a colostomy bag and got it all over our shower until I transferred up to a room with a view of an older British woman with pearls for her neck and breasts across the courtyard. At rehab with me and Harry. The man with the shit bag told me I had girly tits when we lived together. He tried to touch them. I punched his face. I still remember that. I still think that.

They are hairy now, but I guess he was partly right. When I walk around with my wiener low, I think of that. Of how my body isn't pretty like any fighter's. Catherine says she feels awkward standing naked in front of animals. I tell you. I'll tell you. I'll love a woman for that. She is a fully human person with herself intact. Everything that was ever before me I have done the wrong things to or with. She smokes ciggies. She has hair like horses standing in smoke. She steps through Manhattan. She can play Arabian music on recordings for days. I've been everywhere but Africa and China and North Korea and a few others. She is my girl even though she isn't.

See, they move me up to my room. They give me numbers now and IVs.

Amylase 876	Lipase 2660
475	1381
522	?

They come at 4 a.m. or slightly after that and put a needle in my arm. I've asked them to use it in my hand. They've started taking blood from my wrist each morning. It feels so good to be asleep. Then to have a woman wake me up and take my hand, even to stick a vein, take part of me away with her.

Nothing is working and I know why: it's Catherine. I am feeling often like I don't have enough jump in my beans. The truth is I have given too much away. I'm like Christ without his magic. All I got is the side wound. The open heart. The world doesn't want to hear this sort of thing out of me. That man, he probably stretched my first girlfriend to the moon. Men like thinking of things like that. Women, too, some. Why say negroid instead of black? It's unpardonable, but I liked him and he was real and I didn't want to be safe, I wanted to be the one who wasn't privileged. I'll tell you: because it makes *me* wrong instead of right. Right by only saying the right word? Give me a new joke! This is the united America. Pick your common magazine. It's a disaster. Let's not kid ourselves. Using the right words! Don't fiddle my faddle, lesser evil, poppycock. Either way it's peanuts and popcorn. I'm not going to use the right word and perpetuate the wrong stereotype. I wish it were easier to take. I could have said person of color, as this happened, and then what? Then who's safe.

Everywhere my Catherine and I went, men had urges for her. She's in New York. She says to me last week, a woman like me in a town like this, and she smiles, which I can hear over the telephone line, then giggles. You should see what a class act she always is. The kind who won't let you in the room while she's taking a pee. Always locks the door. Always hose and perfect dresses. Ties around the waist. Little ears and earrings and that neck on her. Always with some new terrifically brilliant thought to share, a viewpoint to take you to see it—a church in the West Village with a hole in its giant door you can see to a quaint unmowed lawn of fallow grasses, a few old headstones, a smell of fresh earth, right in the city, her in a dress. I could get sick all over again, the world still moving, never a second of peace from Yours Truly for Yours Truly, and Catherine shows us heaven on earth.

See, a few days now and they got my case figured out finally.

I got drinking man's disease. Pancreatitis. The banana above the gut is inflamed. All I can do is lie around and not eat and wait. They give me a suppository. Hard as Hell to peel. I get it free and run it under cold water, crouch in my robe, slip it up inside.

You know who used to want to play with my hole? Catherine. She was always rubbing it while she would please me. Well, and enough of that. I get shy telling her secrets and using her name. Why do I do it? For sound. And for feeling.

Sue me.

Funny I got drinker's disease after all these years without a whiskey. I can't take the good drugs because of sobriety. Well, a little bit here and there I slip out of the nurses. But for the most part, it's just Hell and waiting. Catherine doesn't call. I'm getting older. The old cripple died in her sleep with nothing doing on my part, of course. They don't let me eat. Did you hear what happened to the old cripple? I can't drink water. I smoke in the shower here and the nurses know my tricks. Chew a sponge. Catherine is the most beautiful part of me I have ever had removed. I can't believe I still got to let her go. Feels like I am just touring the facilities here. Next time, though, it will be for keeps. They'll take me and keep me and put me down. All my skin will then be in the game. This time I am lucky, I suppose. The suppository is kicking in and the world is opening back to me like a morning glory in the sphincter of evening.

The light through the window. I'm just waiting to get another round of trouble lined up. I'll never get over her, you know? You know that? Hey, you want to know, hey look? You're looking. You're looking.

THE ADVENTURES OF EAGLE FEATHER

I FOUND a feather the other day. It was from a great Bald Eagle, Christ. I had seen its nest at the top of a dead tree up top. I went asking for the feather for my old man.

My brother and me walking around doing nothing. Me? Post-peyote, head in birds, talking to God and thinking of America.

I thought I'd ask to get an Eagle Feather from the Bald Eagles we saw flying high, the nest up at the top of a living ponderosa dead up top, in the Oregon desert. I was visiting my Oregon home from New York where I'd met Catherine, studied with that old Indian Jew nut, was trying to figure out how to talk. I should have been watching my big and only brother I had, connecting, but I never knew how to do anything. I was raised crazy in a crazier home. I got hit, strangled, beat, knocked the block off, and these were the people who loved me, still love me, tall man I am, have proved themselves and their love and worth, us all broken, me never to stop, I tell you, no sobber story here from me, but I was crazy from the word bananas and coming out of the mother's you-know-what. Vagina. The start of starts. I thought I was an Indian Native all my childhood. Still do. I think I'm from heaven most of the time. I don't know what to do here. I feel myself fading and coming back. Everyone says I need to get ahold of myself. Accept that this is my life. Well, and be serious. Be smart.

Well, I'm flying out of my brain while in my body and I'll tell you, writing this book isn't smart, since too much is true. I'm with old Dennis Hopper, saying, "My written history is one big lie. I mean I can't even believe my own history." So don't you believe it. I'm very much here but not, because I buy my own lies. So I need sex and sex and food and cigarettes and hands and skin and my arms and the wild look of the words moving and shimmering after not coming back right from being with Natives on Peyote. And I wanted to get that feather to send to my teacher. So I could really figure out how to get more real. You know? To know I was who I thought I was, an Indian Kid, a great white Indian peyote writer. And guess what? The feather came to me right as I asked.

I dropped tobacco from a cig I took apart and kept the loose stuff in my palm, and I circled the tree counter clockwise, like the turn of the earth, and dropped the tobacco staring up in the tree and praying, like an old wide-faced (I)ndian showed me to do in rehab in the snow in Minnesota around a big oak tree, horses in the field of night, snowflakes falling like drunks, like a dream, stars holy above, and as I finished dropping the last speck, finishing a circle around the ponderosa, praying for the old man in the Upper East Side to have, there it was, standing up in a rich grass, by its quill, right out of the ground. Get it? EAGLE FEATHER. This is a wild trip. Animals come to me now after the peyote. Think of that fox showing up last chapter. I'm a Catholic. As a professor, I say to my students when they ask, that I'm a psychedelic Totem Catholic. That's big in Baptist towns in the South. Religion. There are more animals that come to me. I've been terrified too. Don't get me wrong. That's what's wrong with me. Terror all the time, and living so aware and capable of seeing the walls move, all the time, they move, everything freaking filling with light, forget "capable," the walls bending and everything covered in visible heat, which took years to work out, worrying about God and having terror and having been through too much, or just the right amount, so, well, I can't ever remember the month or what semester I'm teaching in—won't end this sentence with a preposition.

My father (or not my father, but the great man I am speaking of as if he is my father) is how many years old, and smokes how many packs of cigarettes a day. This is me admitting how stupid. How I idolized the son of a bitch. And for what? Is he Jesus Christ? The old Jew? Has he done anything much to change the outcome of the ball game? Zilch, hardly. Still, he made an impression. He has nearly always got an erection when I see him and spends most of his time making up lies to tell whenever I call, or someone phones him, or I think of him getting a telephone call. He's old but it seems like an act. He's lived his LIFE in capital letters. Or can talk like one who has. This isn't my father but my old teacher I got that feather for. He doesn't bathe, except in milk and vinegar and I suspect sometimes he's got other children than me that he won't tell me about. He says I am the only one he's got, ever, and I just wanted to send him the feather along with a rock that I would write we're related on it.

You know it's a federal offense—keeping a Bald Eagle's feather—unless you are a true Injun? It is. Plus, sending them through the mail. I am not a "true" Indian but I am better than a white person. I shoot off .45s in the nude on state lands. I have been with underage women, recently. Plus, I almost always like to masturbate while driving—through the pants.

I think a lot about my old man.

[Newsflash! I've done the white man peyote walk for seven years plus. Meaning I can't see right and I'm haunted by things that I do not understand, having blown my head and flesh wide open on the peyote paste with Indians circled around me in a teepee with feathers in hair and hand drums and old ancient chants which I think is just crying and getting it back together, and the grey ash of creation spinning out around the fire in timeless time pretime on the paste with the spinning ash like star matter making the universe—OH and fear—I still walk and talk and write and dress in a coat and tie and teach University English classes as an Assistant Professor in Baptist country Texas. Don't get me wrong, I'm still a Catholic in the age of the internet and drone aircraft. I'm still up and at it! Bring the cocksuckers, Cocksuckers. It's all confused. Plus I've lost a plotline. I like a cigarette. The smoke in my lungs before blowing it all out. I belong in a poncho eating beans storing my life away in some canvas hutch on a hillside and crying into a woman's old nish, speaking babble and waiting for Christ to appear. I'm trying to open my senses. Or close them. Get ahold of myself. But it's a life, and once you've lost someone like we have, you go on despite it. You make do without your due. You find holiness in the holes where time cuts you a break. You don't count beans, you eat beans. This is America today. No one is fooling anyone, except a lot of people fooling themselves. You'll see who we lost. May you never lose.

I'll tell you this, I like to hit an AA meeting wearing my denims across town here in Texas where I live and hear some people tell some real stories. Light up my light stories. I'll see little angels in the sky inside the building, in the air, little silver dots, and I'll shoot gold out of my forehead, but all I want is to be off this planet in the next world and the next. I've never been comfortable. Except on a wild tear, like you're about to hear with this finding the feather business.]

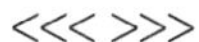

I was driving over the mountains earlier (in the time of the story, before I added these parentheticals) [also brackets, of course] and I got this sense to throw the feather out the window. Everything smelled like hot pine and sun and I started thinking about the feather. I took it out of the glove box and saw it had a white star on the stalk and was otherwise black with a white middle. The softest fluff was down at the base. I was doing how many miles an hour with the windows up. I rolled the windows down, and threw it to the wind. To the hot pine and sun.

My father (see earlier) still lives in New York City. He is sure all the time that he is dying or going to, but he wants to live on terribly. I am in Oregon throwing the feather. I am in Oregon. To Hell with him if he doesn't know how much I loved him. I'd always loved him. The Eagle had done its work. Molted. And I just couldn't stand the thought of the feather going to a place with all that much grime. The taxis all dented up and yellow. The noise and the crowding. I have lived in New York City. The endless endless. The edge. Old man I'm calling father up up in the Upper East Side. He is there with a marble table in a room I've never seen, or in the bedroom with his face in the nishy, womankind still better than us.

I stopped at the ice cream parlor near Detroit Lake for an iced espresso.

"Can I get some room in that," I said to the lady. There was nothing but room for states and states over. This was the wide West.

How much, the lady said.

"How much room you want?" she said. There was a lake outside, Detroit Lake, and pine trees hot in the sun.

"Just enough to stick my whole head in," I told her, and she laughed.

"Never give them a straight answer," I said. "They don't want one."

"What do they want?" she said. She was old and looked skeptical.

"What's the last point you had you any man?" I said.

She gave me the look.

I looked her back in the same way.

We went behind the ice cream cooler and she slipped off her pants. When we were finished, she shut up the store and we went out to my car. The Bald Eagle nested in the back seat. Upholstery had been torn apart, and the foam and springs were all out in the sun.

The windows had been left down. It was my fault, To Hell with it, then. We started driving fast for New York City. When I turned around, I saw the Eagle's feathers flapping in the wind. His wings were spread across the back seat. Now, here's a worthwhile enterprise I figured: 100,000 dollars per Bald Eagle feather and a year in jail each. We were all facing serious charges. The Eagle most of all. He wasn't an Indian, either. Plus my not having a license to drive, if we made it to New York we would be our own heroes I decided and the old woman would become my wife; she'd be pregnant, too. (Catherine and I weren't together yet, but had been some.)

Watch out Pappa. We are coming. And we're never going to stop. Watch out you old head of white hair. We are never going to stop and then we are turning back for the West. To hell with it all, I shouted. To Hell with this having to die. Here comes your boy, Pappa. Here comes your boy—and Hot Pine, and Bald Eagle, and the Old Sexpot right alongside. We are never going to stop—any of us. We are never going to die. Here comes your boy. Here comes all what you have made.

DRUNK AND NAKED
AS HE WAS

IT WAS TIME to play the cowboy. One got a ranch at the end of a long road, a hundred acres of flat, and then got a dog. One was he. (He was me, why pretend?) He (why say he again? I'll tell you why: to give the old "I" word a break.)—he found a posting. The dog was female, to be killed the next day, the posting said. Or put into a killing shelter. She looked lucky. He decided to go and see.

There was this old man with shaky hands who had been the man's friend. He wore a wide hat and leathery pants, oiled and stiff, made of oiled canvas. He was handsome and told great stories of long ago when the world was the man's world. He was a brilliant liar, but the truth was his every word rang true. The old man told one story that always stuck in the new cowboy's brain. It was like a golden lonesome American splinter in there. The splinter worked its way around as the fake cowboy drove the country, which was going from shit to shittier, and found a ranch to rent and now he was going to look at a dog. This was East Texas.

The story with the dog is another story. Needs told. The dog is central to this thing (the book). Everyone has a good dog story.

The old man's story with a dog was that the old man had his second wife and an apartment with fine wooden floors in the California sun, and had decided to paint, or do some varnishing, but had to cook up something on the stove as preparation, or maybe he was smoking, or both? Does one cook varnish of a certain kind? Those old hands back when they were young and handsome, they lit a fire, then added water. The thing spread. Life gets out of hand. He had a dog, an apartment, a wife, and a fire. He ran through the apartment yelling for the dog. The dog and only the dog. This was the old sort of lying. He let the wife fend for her life and went for his dog. But this isn't my story to tell. I should stop. It belongs to another man, but I'll tell it anyway. I'll steal it. It goes like this: the old man was yelling and whooping for Cody, Cody, Cody—the old dog he loved more than her.

The new cowboy found the apartment where the people lived who had the dog. They were not his types of people. The woman was overpowering. The young man of the couple sat with his hands in his hands, failed and failing.

The puppy was a runt with a busted leg that had healed. Her name was Jewely—the puppy's name was. The woman wanted one hundred and fifty dollars to rehome her. This was the predicament, to save the dog or not. Her man wanted whatever the woman wanted. It was a little pup. The new cowboy had never heard of rehoming fees. The dog was otherwise going to be put in a kill shelter, the woman said. Varnished. Cooked. The new cowboy had had a dog, once, all his own, but it'd run away. He'd never had a wife. His true love had just left for a trip to Europe.

The dog Jewely wasn't his kind of dog, but he drove around with her after, and he'd paid the money. She would not look at him. He got her home and they entered his newly rented ranch, which was old to the owner and didn't matter at all to the owner's deceased wife. He put on one of their records. He danced with his shirt off and Jewely yipped and ran over the old floors and slid a little. She was tiny. He fed her hunks of a huge ham and she became a better dog all at once. She was four months old, or three, and had one blue eye and one brown eye. The dog chased him around the house. He had a drink and a cig and danced the entire side of a country western album and the dog chased him around. Then he fed Jewely the rest of the ham she could eat.

But in the story that the old man had told, the one that stuck in the new cowboy's mind, the old man had been young and in New York City. He had gone to a fine clothing store where he'd bought himself a great golden corduroy suit. The suit was ribbed and had big lapels and large brown buttons. There was something else about the suit the young cowboy could never recall, which the old man had told—still with the suit in its fantastic box, he went and picked up his fiancée and they drove to marry in the desert. Then life got out of hand, even that very consummate night. If you want to know more, contact the man who lived it. Upper One Side. New York, New York.

Getting the picture? How it's me and him, but in the end he's out of the picture.

The next night after getting the dog, the new cowboy unpacked all of his boxes of things he'd driven with from New York.

He brought them into the ranch house and unpacked the boxes while Jewely watched. He found a barrel out by some pens and started a fire in his sand yard inside that barrel with all of his old boxes. It burned high and very near the house. Jewely chased charred bits of cardboard and the new cowboy was happier. Ash spread in the wind. It was snowing soot in East Texas.

On the carousel horse, reflected in the mirror, later on, inside the trailer/house, not drunk but drunk, he saw the bit and pliers and cinchers on the carousel horse in the mirror and thought of the woman who had lived in this old trailer he rented, who was dead. Her perfume still on a shelf. He still had all his family living. He meaning I. I, of course, I. He looked at himself. I did. He was just a naked crazy man in a room looking at himself in the mirror. Here was youth gone nearly. He could not remember the word that the old man had used regarding the suit. I still cannot. Catherine and I were still together and Carl was living.

BOOT OF THE BOOT

IF I EVER meet a man named Manuelo from Paris, he'd better watch his fucking head. I mean it. I told her one day when I was soaked with rain, in a white shirt stained brown from shoulder to opposite hip, from a cheap leather strap wet from the rain. I was using the strap to hold a bag with my belongings in it. It needed to be said. I'd been walking in rain lost talking, talking to myself, appearing at an art opening in NY to meet Catherine, and each past boyfriend of hers came by to shake my wet hand. Each one looked at me and stifled a gasp, a laugh, a crack—I gripped her elbow, staring at her ex's tie clip, and said, "Never make me shake hands. If we don't make it, don't you ever introduce me. You hear me? I don't want to be anybody's former anybody. Please, don't make me shake a damn hand. I might not give it back." Giving her some credit, I wasn't easy to be with.

I looked through a very expensive telescope in a grocery store parking lot tonight, and saw what's out there.

And it's impressive!

I mean in space.

I saw the craters of the moon in blinding bone white brilliance, rippling in light and I don't know what. But rippling and bone white right into the craters was mostly enough.

I saw Saturn.

This is not a metaphor. This is not about Manuelo and whatever he is doing over there with Catherine in the boot of the boot. Can you imagine what he is doing with her? In Italy! Christ!

(This is all what I felt and wrote while living at the new ranch only a few months and Catherine went off with a Spanish man named Manuelo who she'd met in Paris, where she was visiting during living for a few months in Italy after I moved to Texas, and we were still together, and I felt it, the moment he touched her and I somehow knew it, what had happened, while staring at St. Jude's Chapel's mural, sitting down to coffee and steak and eggs in Dallas, and later found out, and the times matched up, and I fell to writing this all down.)

I tried to give the man anything. Anything. Food, bottles of wine, sushi, my home to stay in. He wanted nothing—the man with the scope.

I want to tell you about the man with the scope. I mean to tell you what is out there around us in space. I want to tell you about her.

Catherine. Her name is like space and what there is unto itself that I saw out there. Last time I told it I showed her all wrong—in the wrong light. Last time, she came back and we went to Puerto Rico. We saw wild horses. We swam in the dark before the moon rose to swim and the water lit up wherever we swam and made glowing dots green on our skins in the dark. We had rode a motorbike all over the island, me driving too fast, as fast as it would go over the wild, bumpy, bare earth to the sea to swim in a bioluminescent bay full of sharks. Her dark hair and pale skin and a vein dark across her unknown heart.

I was held up at gunpoint by a man in Puerto Rico and the man who held me up had tears in his eyes. I made him give me a cigarette after I gave him my money, which wasn't much. I had thought about punching him, since it was just me and him, and he was bleary eyed, leaning against a palm tree on a motorbike, but I just made him light my cigarette. He was so Christian about it. Him crying for robbing me in the dark. He had a great .45. Catherine was back in the room, naked under the sheets. I was six and a half feet tall, searching, white fake Indian cowboy, with the world going two thousand m.p.h. around itself at any given point, and the peyote in my senses for six years so far, as I went cooling through my pants and sky and the world and I made that sonofabitch light my cigarette and he cried and circled me in his hidden drugged pain. For the shame of not carrying his pain without the drugs, maybe he cried. I was still overcoming pancreatitis. (There's more to this story. This was before Texas, after the hospital, before Manuelo.) He had his friends come over from across the street where they'd hid in the dark. Back then I felt if I stared anyone in the eyes they could see my inner self, straight from the peyote, could see I was the real genuine leather. Now I'd be afraid and serious. They tried to translate but I already spoke Spanish. I'm talking about he who robbed me and lit my cig and his friends from across the street. They were so sad when they heard about the pancreatitis. I made the mistake and told the crying robber I didn't want the rest of his cigarettes because I was getting over pancreatitis. They said the word pancreatitis like the last part of the word was *titties*. I felt so foolish, smoking, as a cop drove past and I signaled I was doing fine.

She won't come back this time. (Catherine. It's been years.)

[I went on my first date after Catherine, and the woman's tooth had broken in half the night before. She kept the date and stuck the tooth, the broken away half, up in her gumline to hold it in there. It was one of her front ones. She kept excusing herself to the bathroom. With dinner served, it kept falling out and she would say, "My tooth. My tooth!" and cover her mouth with her hand and relocate to the bathroom for repair. During the meal, it (her tooth) kept falling out into her creamy pasta and she would search and dig for it with her fork. I took her home by cab after the dinner during which her half (tooth!) kept coming out, remember, and she would return to the bathroom and return to the table. I was embarrassed, but as a man, you know, you can't just leave. You can't just say, "I'm sorry, this isn't working. I am going to go home." There are certain performances, you know, for everyone, and we aren't all animals, us animals. She tried to get me to kiss her wildly in the cab. I wish I could say I had wildly kissed her. That I had kissed her and gone mad with passion. I kept thinking about Catherine and what I was doing in exchange for losing her. Fink I was. I should have thought, what a girl! So willing and ready to see me she comes with a broken tooth stuck up within the gumline.]

I moved into the ranch house full of a family's things. There's pictures of boys with big ears on a wall. One wall has a cutout of Texas made from yellow wood, with varnished little shelves. On a clothespin glued into a tin of an old heat lamp is a sign made many years ago. It says, *Mother my darling Mother my dear...I love you...I love you...each day of the year.* There is a candle in a drawer, shaped as an 8. There is a bottle of Norrell perfume in the bathroom and photos of people who came from Mother my darling, Mother my dear, and I am not from this family. I rent this home. The Mother my darling is dead as can be.

Catherine is hard and keeps herself to herself and everyone who sees her sees she is hard but there is something else to Catherine. She has a child inside her—a girl who may have written the sign from the shelf on the wall. She hasn't lost that. She is intact. She can write, too. Have anyone. What a beauty full of brains and a good heart, but I said I would show her this time. Anything went wrong with me, she'd say, "I think it's a good thing," and then tell me why. She would hold my ear to cool us down. She put up with me being insane in NY, smoking, on nicotine patch systems, chewing drugged gums, running too many miles in all directions snapping on my forehead with my fingers and dressed in the same clothes every day, panicking with visions in NYC. We moved to my family's home in Oregon in the desert. We bought lingerie and had fires. She took to running. Her hardness has kept the child in her alive, maybe, along with her immense beauty, or she isn't hard at all but I made her so with me (first chasing her around before and after classes with the old man in the hat, then when I was with her and cowering in New York in her room, smoking up all night with fear from exhaustion and so in love with her while she just tried to sleep, me talking and moaning and putting it in her with her sleeping, thinking and sensing with my corpus something evil all around in the buzzing city night, me: up, up, up. In love with the old man with the feather in the city with the city in America with America! She and I both working to be true.) Manuelo must see her, now. I wanted to make her pregnant and have a live baby. I once or twice or every time came inside her with hope we might make life without her consent—to carry on the great family. Hers and mine, both.

There was and is a church in the town where I grew up and at the front is a mural in gold squares and blues and reds and greens and it is Jesus with a pierced side bleeding and the blood turns to fire and the fire into wine in a chalice and from the chalice doves appear and fly upwards in rippling white. My parents married in the church. I was baptized in the church and I loved the church and later I became afraid of the church and loved the church as well.

(My brother was baptized there too. We wore the same lace gown. He then I. We were like little Christs and grew side by side toward our trouble making heartfelt lives. We had our differences of course. We didn't stay two by two. We each had our path, but by the end and the way through we never turned a back. We always loved one another. In the end and all through he loved me and let me grow up the way I did, into the thing I am, the man, if you want to say that, and I always felt and feel he was the secret greatest. There's more of him to come! [He died at 33, year I am now.] I cannot believe he has gone on, rode on ahead, not here with us, me, crazy, and my family, dead. But I wrote this before he left.)

(I smoked a strange drug with an Indian when I was a younger man and went back to the church ((on the drug)) in Ohio with my spirit. You leave your body on this drug. I saw the stained glass windows pinwheel with light and geometry.

They were always beautiful in physical presence. But this was warmth and light not from the sun through glass but from God, or from the soul of the self, the universe, from the tomahawk of what was loaded up for me in that pipe, which the brain lets rip when you die, which also makes you dream, and there was no anxiety of being—anxiety that being separate from the universe is the source of all pain and suffering—I wasn't separated. I felt God beside me and in me and I in It. Looking without the eyes. Feeling God behind the poker face. I felt the world after death and it is beyond impressive! Hours later a car flew off a cliff before the rig I was in, which had a driver who'd picked me up hitching. Who had one leg but never mind that, the driver's half leg. This was real life. The car that flew off the road landed at a forty-five degree angle and nose planted in the river, standing on its grill in the water like an enormous arrow. I rushed down a herder's path and held a boy alive and in shock and felt parts of him go soft. He looked into my eyes, which back then were clear and I showed anyone. Others had come down switchbacks from the road high above. "You're doing fine," I told him. I felt the easiest sense of calm. Old God and me looking into him with great affection. A helicopter came out of the sky. Times like that the world isn't doing too bad in America. Boys and girls coming down in a helicopter to save him and his girlfriend, she in worse shape, who knows if she lived. He did, I believe, but her, who knows. They lifted them into the sky. There we were, finding our own way home from then on and forever. I was sort of wearing a half dressed outfit, by this time, and the man with the half leg had me drive him to the Mission in San Francisco, my golden town. The driver, now I'll tell you, had lost half his leg in a single nod off on junk. Circulation. Me in a half dressed state, barechested in youth. When he scored and shot, what was I still doing there? He filled the center chute with his own blood mixing with the junk. I guess I wanted to see it live, and then he shot some up to the sky. There was, on the ceiling of the RV he drove, blood and brown from before. What was my cue? Arrivederci, I was off, and not to cocksucking Italy.)

Sometimes I get to thinking of her over there with Manuelo and Italy and how it's every girl's dream to go to Paris and fall in love and then I get in my little rig and drive to walmart in town and walk around at 2:00 or 2:23 a.m. and look at anyone. Look at all those people. I have seen an odd armadillo in the grass tottering on its legs—and I think of all the men who ever loved and lost and went out to outer space to live with themselves.

Then a song on the radio plays as I drive over the stumpenly remains of a freshskinned skunk torso twisted in the roadway stinking through the boat of my car's undercarriage.

She's over there in Paris with Manuelo. She was visiting Italy only, she said. You have got to love the thing that will not cease itself or be killed or let itself die. Guess that's not us. Once it's gone, how can you love it? Is it something else you are loving then? When it comes to sexual love? Mother my darling...Mother my dear...I love you...I love you.

I picture them in Paris. I have never been there, but I imagine the streets are prettier than here.

In a desk in this home I rent there is a box of Mirado quality writing pencils—the best! There is a small clear sharpening box taped to the box of pencils. Somebody taped that there. Let me tell you, they're the best!

At the grocery store tonight, there was a man with a very nice telescope. He was waiting for fools like me who wanted to look out into space. He moved the position of the telescope and found the moon. I looked into the scope.

I once saw my sister being born. Me and my brother did. I watched a man in a uniform with a scalpel and blood dripped into a silver bowl and I watched my mother scream. Yell, really. Yell and yell. Whoop. Whoop. Whoop. Mother my darling... Mother my dear....

Saturn was so far away, even through the telescope, it looked like a little trick on a screen.

Manuelo isn't half the crazy that I am. I can prove that, too.

Why do you suppose he did it? Why are we so interested in space? Whose stars are those you see at night? Who has got his hands upon Catherine right now? Her skin lit up green in a dark moonless bay? Her whole heart alive. The man with the telescope, his eyes were screwed up like he hadn't spent much time looking at things down here. What do you think makes a man do a thing like that?

BEFORE CARL LEFT

YOU WANT to know how dumb I am, Yours Truly? You want to have any idea what sort of…it's embarrassing. It is. I am ashamed. I mean, this is the sort of dumbshit nonsense that I am talking about. But when I tell you this, you are never going to want to hear from me again. I mean, you will not want to read any of what issues forth from out of me after. None of my harebrained ideas, schemes. You are going to want to cut ties, I am saying. Well here it is. Here's the hair from my brain. It is nothing, really, that you cannot probably get behind. I moved to East Texas. You probably know, I left New England. So long. Left New York City behind. Goodbye. Even as mostly a visitor. A little post teaching and editing on weekends, scratching nothing out. Nothing much. But I moved to East Texas, and started taking up in this little hundred acre ranch. Got some dogs. You remember? A puppy. An older dog, came with the place, too. A third that came over days from the neighbor's trailer. I had to do something with the trash, the garbage. It was the night before a trip. I should tell you, ice storms had wracked the country. Is that the word for ice storms? I'll leave that to the papers' writing and the news people. That's what they are good at mostly, for, the papers. Coming up in verbs having to do with snow, or ice, or weather. Terrorism and what idiots think about everything—reported to the whole world on our new news. You get it, don't you? I'm in the weather like you are also. It was snowing in East Texas. It was not going to be cheap, heating this house. I'll tell you that. There were cheaper years to move to Texas. That's for sure. I don't have a mountain of cash. That is for sure. To rent a hundred acres and heat a house. But it is what it is, right? I figured I needed to have a ranch to be in Texas the way one should be in Texas. I'd lived in the roach and rats buildings in New York City. I wasn't going to get an apartment in Dallas. I was on a ranch with steer that screamed in the night and coyotes in the near distance and Jewely. I had found the Eagle Feather. I was going to always love Catherine regardless. I was a man in the wild world. It's what it is. So, it's snowing and I had all this trash.

I got the goddamn dogs. Got them riled up. I can't find my lighter. I'm yelling at the dogs questions out loud. Gathering up the plastic and the trash, '*And there ain't nothing like a friend who can tell you you're just pissin' in the wind*,' Neil Young was in the room over on the record wheel. (I hadn't lost my brother, Carl, yet. Carl left us a few weeks ago. Over two months ago. (Over one year ago.) Carl is gone. Carl died in his bed. [Two years ago.] There isn't anymore Carl on this planet we are stuck to. Not here, in terms of a body, in terms of our living Carl. In terms of that Carl is my only brother. My older brother.)

So, I got all my papers. I have been having a case with the writing. I would not say blocked. I would never say that. Not that I wouldn't say blocked. Just not about me. I got about two or four hundred or five thousand crumpled papers in a wooden bin for trash in my office—the bin the owner of the ranch's father built. You'll hear about the owner of the ranch's son, Squeaky, soon enough. *Mother my dear*, get it? Is this coming together? Carl? Are we rolling? There are pictures in frames in the office of boys, kids I've never met, the owner's brother's kids—or who knows whose?—break your heart boys: big ears with haircuts and teeth. Anyhow, I got all the papers and trash outside into the fire bucket. I hate to burn plastic, but there was plastic and it had fish in it, and there is no garbage service out in those living fields. Really I do hate to burn it. I found the lighter. I got the fire going. It's curling and smoking. It's nighttime and my puppy is part husky. Part, also, mixed. (Turns out she's not husky, but dingo.) It's her first snow. The smoke from the paper is making a shadow that rolls across the white snow in the pretty dark. It is first like the snow is being blown over the snow. It's really pretty. Carl was still alive, remember? Remember. Then I put the plastic on the fire. I know, but it's Texas. I'm flying the next day. The plastic had fish in it. Other sorts.... So I start praying. I am always praying. I start praying to God to forgive me for the plastic I'm sticking in the ozone. I start praying all over around the fire asking for my words on the pages to be beautiful as they burn, and for the words to be prayers, and for the prayers to lift and overpower the plastic fumes. I start praying for man to be good enough to overcome all the toxic shit. I start praying and then I think Lucifer instead of God at one point and it just turns my guts. It's idiotic. I mean, it's imbecile hour on the ranch. Here I am hoping my words on fire will be prayers lifting in the smoke. And then I think the wrong word, again, and it tears me apart. It's so stupid. I mean it's really dumb.

TOUGH BEAUTY

I AM H. ROC your man, but in love. Meaning I am your man and in love and I am your man except in love. Meaning please figure it out, Cocksucker. Meaning please listen up. Meaning Yours Truly is screwed up and has screwed up on to here, where I am now, which I will tell you *where* if you are good and pay attention—for once. (Where I am has changed. I was in an RV park when I wrote I would tell you where I was, and I still will tell you where I *was*, but now I am in San Diego squatting at a university I never went to school at in a giant RV rig.)

I went to the San Diego Jesuit university church this morning and wept and wept, reaching into the celestial heavens, me who came up with the name H. Roc as an alias, as a fiction, and with this dirty story you are going to read; me in church with my spirit Indian non-Indian, nonhuman self, in church thinking the wrong words from moment to moment, in California, on a hill in a great cathedral, in an architectural heavenly kingdom of Spanish-y mission buildings and gardens, hearing the wrong words in church, the old crazy in me of the old lunatic in me who has seen much with his eyes and heart open and his head miswired and the things I see are tilted to one side and then another, and cannot see a straight line, firing too fast in all lines, but still I reached up into the celestial heavens of the Creator of the Universe, and then had a fifty dollar brunch of crab legs and raw oysters and roasted meat and drank sparkling water orange juice and walked around a graduation ceremony and lived through the families and couples.

Say I am a lost dog with my lost dog, only I am not a dog, and my dog is *my* dog, and I am a man upon the planet who is a family member of all families, but no one wants me, exactly, though I put on a great show of being an acceptable human. Plus my cock is far beyond average and I have a lot of firepower to give. Who wants to be human in these families, anyhow? I'm here. Baby. In California, I am saying, not in the RV park you will read about in a few minutes. Ah scamp!

Squatting in a giant bus, living off the fruit of the land, working around words, in fruit of the looms, in my RV, reading a bit of my old teacher, and remembering the him who no one else knows—because just every stitch and wool and skin and heart of what I know of him is how he presents himself, and how he knows me, saw me, and said to me, *My Boy, it seems you never had a home, but you have earned a home, right here, with me, forever, don't come visit, call here and there, up to my neck in pussy, gotta run, but you're my Boy*, and how many people is he a father to!

Though I am hereby required to strike it big, or strike out, and then I found him the Eagle Feather, which is exactly what the Eagle Feather is for, for the leader who leads with the giant American heart, the great desert West's heart, the giant world heart, the heavenly heart, the perverted heart, the pussy hound's heart, which means you have to love, oh baby, LOVE—the women you are in with—but you don't want to hear this kind of shit from me, you want to hear how I can't not look at the rear ends and the beautiful hearts of gorgeous California tan-legged beauties in Mass, and their noble looking men, and how I think the wrong words in Mass, and how I am a haunted lunatic nut, and how I got that way: partly how it was having a peyote nutcase breakdown, and partly was losing someone I love the most and then really for true losing someone I love far more than that. I dress in the mirror of this long van in my van's bathroom, my motor coach, 31 feet long, 25 years old, smelling of real wood and a shower, and put on my belt and my seersucker pants and my linen shirt and my boat shoes—and then walk around graduation looking at all the families and the money and how tears roll down my face and I am amazed in church, and how I am amazing, and I can't believe how amazing I am and how amazing the world is, and how amazing church is, and how amazing my teacher is, haha, who always wanted to be amazing, an inside joke, and how amazing California, and how I have an image in my head of my old teacher, and me, and all the wildcrackers full of jumping beans of the Lord and these wild mazes of words we have to construct to make the Godhead. And Catherine. But now you're in for this story about my ugliness and my breakfall down into crazy peyote bananas.)

Julie Townlove and guess who had been up by the Interstate Motel? Me! H. Roc. (The Interstate Motel is a real motel on the way to my ranch you now know a portion about. I transplanted the motel to California. Why did I transplant the motel by the ranch out to California? To talk out of my mouth about my youth into a tape recorder while I was driving, years ago. Julie Townlove I made up as a symbol of my youth because she'd love anybody in town. This was my joke about what kind of a girl I was always taking up with back then. Back when a joint in the park meant, dynamite, women galore. I can't hold a candle to knowing a thing about women. A candle is another thing I can tell you about but I won't. Meaning guess who will tell you?

The candles at the table, I used to stare into them and the light and feel myself going out of myself into the room like light itself. Like the candle was my name. I could feel the light in me, I am saying, going out into the room.

Catherine and I had a glimmer of a hope of knowing a thing or two about each other for a couple of years and I still believe we knew one another, but then we had a real hope of being together even with the self I was with her, in her, beside her, feeling we were working our ways toward facing what was there inside us from our respective starts in life, feeling we could sit at a table together and have it be *our* table, but look what happened with me and Catherine! Sayonara as the Spanish say, am I right? Ha! No not that I am angry. I'm astonished. I'm plumb amazed. Astonished she went anywhere with me when I met her in our teacher's class and went out to smoke ciggies, I stationing myself next to her against the outside wall out on E. 47th Street and talking to her despite her body saying she did *not* want to talk to me, but her eyes still considering me. You know what she later told me about what she could smell about me from seven feet away, or six point five? When we would have sex the light would come through us. I'm sure you don't want to hear these stories out of me or watch us in the act.

Know how I got her to come out with me? Here is how. I had a car and she was tired. Her feet! You have heard about her feet! This was in old New York City. Our genius teacher had told stories for six hours without saying um, without boring anyone to tears, while making life better than it had ever been on paper and not even using paper. So, she left me, which I needed, I suppose, to write all this, but I would burn this and be with her if she asks me to burn this and be with her.) [Too late…A joke!]

I'm telling you I was wrong with the Julie Townloves because I was wrong in that I was only in it for myself.

So…we had run and gotten and come back. [I wrote this when Catherine was still in Italy, and me and her writing back and forth and me still thinking I was the one and that I had made it through my idiot youth mania and found "real" life to be with her. Carl still alive. Plenty of heart and will and time ahead. Pancreas healed up and back to banana shape and relative size. Having survived the Indians. Having survived jail and rehab and myself and found myself a grown adult, one who wasn't kidding around anymore, who said "for keeps" all the time and meant it. Still trying to get my talking mind to speak something, something big, something wild and free and in the music of myself, something utterly new in utterance, but being delusional as our teacher called me, after I wasn't there anymore in his class the next year, him in front of Catherine, him referring to things I had written down and sent him in the mail that I had driven myself nuts with at the keys in Spain, when I had taken Catherine on the back of that motorbike, all 50cc's, on the Spanish freeway, which isn't called a freeway, because, guess why? Guess what place isn't a place I would call free? Guess what country and countries, for reasons you will see and have already in part seen, I would not call free? As in, try and start up a conversation with someone there while walking around an old church or museum or in the club? As in, try and find a wild bear or even an eagle or a fox out over a certain landmass where certain white people and darker mostly white people come from and live? As in, guess who doesn't think of himself as being a white person exactly, though he is a white person? You'll hear more about that landmass and what happened that went so wrong to me on that landmass. For now, let's just for Christ let this story finish without any more out of Yours Truly because I don't want to talk anymore. AND you won't hear a word out of me in the next story after this one.]

Only I had not rushed up and gotten and come back with Julie. I had smoked and bit my fingernails and hung my arm out the window, pushed wheel and pulled stick, commanding the driving through the West with the radio cranked with Julie. (Not the dog. This is a different type of story. This is talking about something through something else, remember?)

In the Interstate Motel, her blonde pussy was open with her robe's slip open and Julie was working herself out on the California King—(the person, remember!) and we were both open. Us human kids. The sun through her pink lips and in her open eyes—hair all free from her head but still in her head at one end and rock and roll coming through the radio and freedom galore in a motel with a window.

Oh, to be free and young again in a motel in a wide-open country with animals. Pine trees. The smell of water in summer by a river.

The sun was slicing through the blinds and sitting in a wingback in the room. I was handsome and proud and nervous of the feelings I had inside of me watching Julie in her nudity.

(Guess who I am not talking about? The one I am here to talk about, Carl. Meaning I don't know how to talk about Carl, but I am getting to talking more about him, and here's a hint where yours truly is [was] right now [then] writing this [that]... Tier Drop RV Park. Here's another hint, I'm not mixing one place up with another. Here's another hint: when someone dies there is often money left over in policies. Here's another hint, that makes a person who lost his best first friend and only brother want to cry in the RV park and guess who has the old wet face? Guess, what? Who did I call when I landed back from Europe with a brother not living anymore, my only brother, who is better than I am and I talk to at nights driving alongside a train on Hwy 8 with a light on and the engine going and me going and going on to nowhere, someplace else, and when cresting a mountain with a radio tower so planes don't hit the mountain? Guess who was on a plane and standing at the back of the plane and looking at the exit and going nuts inside himself—who was considering opening that plane door and going out of the life like the only person I ever knew who was my brother and would say, You're good, I love you, I'm proud of you: you just worry too much, you just have anxiety, there's nothing wrong with you. I was in Europe when I got the phone call. Thought it was the motorcycles first off. Howling and screaming.... I cannot tell you what this was like. How it haunts me: that moment in that room. Just a room. That pause before I heard what I was told I needed to sit down for to hear. How much I can't tell you about him. How the whole world could have sooner been blown to Hell, was what I thought for the first year after. Over and over. Guess who took me in a cab when I couldn't breathe out of a place where everyone was going nuts to rock and roll and said to the cab driver, with his arm around me, my brother's giant warm arm, said, "This is my brother. I love him. I want you to take us to such and such address?"

Guess who was shaking because he was about to open that airplane door except he had to get home to take care of what had to be taken care, which was not what should have been taken care of, because I didn't take care. I called the old teacher when I got to the ground, pacing up and down the airport, hyperventilating, throwing up inside, having no idea what to do, having bought everyone presents, having done the unthinkably wrong thing of buying everyone presents. Just a man in the face of the unthinkablest personal tragedy, falling back on old habit, buying presents, coming home not empty handed, but by God, can you imagine buying presents, can you imagine!

The old man answered my call. He knew my name by voice. He was a pin a thousand miles into the earth holding me to the ground when the door of the plane was not opened and still I was falling. Guess who said what needed to be said? Guess who can't tell you what that train feels like with that light on standing on the side of the highway on the track? You know what it is like to sit with your brother, after all the bananas of growing up in a crazed home with crazy people, and facing the world, and crashing the mind, and never having been in the right mind in the first place, and two brothers and a sister sitting together in Hawaii, which you will hear about, one sober, two drinking, and just sighing a breath of life out into that tropical air and laughing after a shit wedding of our mother, and feeling like there were two people who you really knew and who you could feel inside you? I'm pissed off about how much

I know about the stars and stripes. You cocksuckers in Europe! Get a bear. Get two bears, male and female, and get them to fuck each other.)

So, I was roasting a smoker toasting up California and its fruited plain and Julie's fruit was shining and we were rich and I felt the sunshine on the carpet's plaid pattern and on the checkered wallpaper and also on the pictures behind glass of the shadow and dogs hunting in the woods. Oh dream of the alabaster city, as we were just above it as in America the Beauty. Liberty was our nakedness and my knife was across my chest because I liked it there. There was nothing but time and freedom.

Julie was sitting up talking about the pure dream of land, her hair free and some pasted to her forehead with sweat. Julie was on her back working out the details of buying land. My American hard-on was soon standing up for itself, big and proud.

In that motel was the start of all things—I thought I could get away with living. I'd grown up in the woods peeing in little holes, stalking the trees and watching through soft vision for tan deer I did not see but saw in my mind. Seeing the road too the first time. Then I had taken the road alive a few years after. I had not kin like-minded for figuring life out. They were crazed in the home, in the oak and hickory, and I was in the motel with Julie Townlove as a young man and we had money and were near enough to the Pacific northern coastline, but not trapped against the ocean with nothing but sand and water to stare at or sleep to—alive and firing—just above the golden dream of the alabaster city on the hill in Northern California.

Sitting in the motel wingback, I could feel through the walls—the sun and sky. Pure peace and meditation. The sort of blue the sky was I was feeling out into the redwoods of the valley, sensing bridges trembling in traffic in the golden city, and the old veterans in bushes near the hill, like bears, like wildmen keeping the country going even still, maddogging the old city, growling, shouting around about remembering Fort Knox, live generals, field armies, air strikes, Marilyn Monroe, terrifying us all, and I could happily hear a tit or two harden in valleys between here to NYC, of Midwestern girls and their mothers, in training bras and big silk brassieres with hooks and straps and eyelets and lace trimming and big pads, as nothing was beyond me, I'm saying I could still feel and sense so far out I could let myself go all the way sitting in the wingback and letting the air move through my blood—I could hum, I say, loving all to the sun. (I used to meditate, transcendentally, and still do in the front of the RV. That light from the candles, from the sun, from Something a million thousand miles away and right here, that's still with old odd me. I sit up front near the engine hub in my 1988 RV and hum but it's all kind of broken.) Yes, I felt God inside me in the motel, Him agreeing with how agreeable I was to the easy law of Yes. I was like flat water moving through the valley of the yellow sun—or some such picture. Deep still water, like that old song describes and says things best as songs can and must do. Like happy plants with fine names.

Next, we are on a farm but not farming vegetables.

Harvest and I was a tall wreck of nerves and bandits came. We were dope farming. Dope. Do I have to spell it out to you? I fished out my pistola and got nervous and shot one bandit through the foot or it was a plant. Another escaped my .44 Vaquero shot, but twisted up his ankle and limped off the side of the hillside trotting and whining. I had one bad boy, all of 19 or 19½ or no more than 19¾ and I got mad and busted his mouth out with the butt of the revolver and sent him away, him bleeding with broken teeth and gums and his tongue twisted up like a dark small foot in his mouth.

First thing, Julie is set on spending our time on Reservations. She's had enough talk of my youthful Injun visions, and wants to see what was before white people such as us. What was woman to me but wanting more than the sham of self I created all alone with her growing pot plants the size of tubas on a hillside in the red California dirt?

We were with the Indians drinking beers on the rez in a tin ranch. Then them to whiskey the two fat cousin braves and a pair of kissing girls, their sisters, in thick hair, making the boys snicker. What are we doing why? Julie has picked up a case of lice and I have a young beard growing crazy all over my neck and cheeks and ears. The darkness in the shack is growing and I'm drinking cola, waiting outside for us is the sun with the blinds drawn. I am still wearing the knife but their dog is growling, and they are skunked. We are having a good time, but it's a trap—like most things native, I speculate, from the little I've seen hotdogging around the planet in cuttoffs and something stupid looking as a banana yellow midriff. I don't trust the Indians when it comes to spending time together, and that's only a feeling I have for the shade they live in is/was from our terrible white doings and our openness in the time of our time on the earth. They are covered in their secret sitting and being calmly dark featured, and their history is a thing blood kept, but in their historical minds nothing but landscapes or bloodbaths, how can I know?

We stay like this a long time with a great clay pot on the table with four cacti of knowledge, their white heads crowned and humming with power. We gobble them through the long lip of unspooled night. We eat in ceremony, but I'm still terrified stupid. They chant and drum and you can hear only parts of their praying but understand it in its totality. Injuns! It is a great and evil sin what we did to them, but somehow we just forget it as part of the premise of our own minds? The peaceful Indians. Or they were always killers, or it varied tribe to tribe, I'd have no real way of knowing. My breathing is chopped and I have stepped into something I should not have. There is no airplane or helicopter door out and no time. Worlds warping, preying dark. Here is rebirth, horrid to watch I'll tell you. A coward in ceremony is no friend to anyone.

Then something's in my eyes and there's a blur over all I see and it feels false. The Injun spirits start crowding us. We're dripping, Julie and I, or it's just me. All across the wall's heat are savage demons of pretime's dawn dawning on me. Each bird is headless behind my closed eyelids for years after, but animals come to me in my open-eye time. A slant-eyed Fox, or a young Coyote, or Eagle or Hawk or Mountain Cat. My eyes can't see them right, though, so I am on the earth sucked into it and come back out ugly and the people are awful and death and walking dead with extended tongues. The knife is on my chest, weakly. We're both dripping in shadows and hell everywhere. For daylong to years passing it's grey flesh and the memory of better times with my spirit as it was like a chapel in the bone desert church of New Mexico now gone—but only a place of human hair voodoo relics and fear in my upper neck and back. Ever since, I am nervous and can't smoke dope right or drink.

Soon, Julie's mating with an Indian from across the dirt, and dogs growl at her heels, and her crotch is full of crud and curds and she's hiding a great sorrow or evilness, or I am wrong. She'd held me and then did not. I saw the sun on the path and the sun was not the sun but the memory of the sun. No horses to ride. We had no motel. I didn't like anyone. I got frantic.

The Injuns had taken it as theirs. Everything!!!... We had to sit and listen at their talks. I had dreams while awake. Then Julie took down with a guy from the rez for a spring term of rez community college and I find out—I mean she'd been fucking him after history. I take the chief's compound bow and arrow and am hunting the Ponderosa restaurants where her fat Indian likes to eat, feathers black hanging from the stave of the chief's bow, only my brain is trash and I might not be there at all. I got moments of rock and roll and rivers and delight, then back into blurry torment.

Julie Townlove's in this Ponderosa where I also am, with her brave Injun she's been fucking and they are at the salad bar loading up the chow. Her blonde hair and bent ears. Miniature corns and spinach meatloaf and broccoli dripping and cheese sauce in baked potatoes and metal canisters of soup. Salad tongs, and I am going to kill that Injun, or at least arrow one of his legs.

Slipping inside the can, I loop up the bow and unfold my folding arrow from a bag. I am stalking like the boy I once was in the woods, but am outside the restroom in the restaurant on the carpet barefoot as a barefoot man. I'm squeezing my legs together around a bottle and I'm squeezing my guts and I know how far I will go, which is all the way, or at least for the leg. Inside my pants is fruited hooch. It is for Julie for after I kill the Indian, or pop him in one leg, one of them, of his two, whatever! There is only liquor and darkness, and the things of the world I wish still held the light but do not. I hid behind a vinyl booth.

Her man sat down and I drew the bow back and rose up on one knee. I hefted over a booth back and steady handed I let it rip. My fart releases itself and I cough and choke and one evil spirit released from me, and do I feel better? Less even though I aimed for the savage's lower parts, the arrow gores his brain and he flops back in his booth screwing up at the air, humping up to death. Julie curses my name, by the wrong name, and spits on the carpet, and the people eat and we get out. Only, where is the Ponderosa?

We kiss with our bodies and mouths.

I pushing into her in the parking lot bushes by the curb down in the mulch and cigarette discards and chewing gum chewed balls and her pushing back. Pulling back while she's grunting, "You sonofabitch," she says, pants and panties around her ankles, "Human," she moans, bees in her hair, I sense—buzzing. "Anyhow, time is running, ruining you like we all could have guessed," she goes. "You've never had any love and when you find love, too old, who even cares if you'll be fine. You're irrelevant." I looked down at Julie and one of her two eyes had nearly popped out, she'd grown yellow skinned and horrible and humping her I come to grips with what I'm doing wrong. Right as I'm about to let myself squirm, I pulled out and took myself mean-groined to a U.S. recruiting station, and signed up to the Afghan mountains because I had no idea and was scared to go to jail for the Indian's murder, if I murdered anyone? Who knows what was what anymore? No one. I had lost track of which side of the tracks I was ever on, in terms of the sound mind. I didn't know when the last time I had really truly seen Julie was anyhow? That all had or hadn't happened? And what was left in or of America? I was going to the army.

I had camo and a beltpack—and a commercial plane ride to the Mid-East. I'm in it and up and there's no getting off the ride. No retreat! the recording on my headphones repeats. No surrender! "I hear you!" I shouted on the plane. I didn't know how loud since I was wearing earphones.

After Air America, I was on my way to kill with a gun and my eagle knife strung across my chest. Yes, I have always known luck. I still don't see like a person, but I feel many fine things such as when I see poor people having small fires by a lake, or a child in happy slowedness, or quickness. Music, too, often affects me. A stone building built in the old fashion in a desert makes me feel patriotic and I at times see the sky correctly. It's amazing how much you can surmount and keep going once it's too late.

On the main service road, over there, with our boys, fire fired up. You'd think that in a war men can shoot clean, but they cannot, Lord. The women either. Everyone is missing everyone. In the fallout of some blown-apart office building I see silver tears coming from my forehead. Then the helicopters come like the drums of the Injuns, and I am shaking and praying to sky. Dragons appear, only not dragons, fierce little Apaches, great compact brown Boeing bastards—weaponized shit-hawks from McDonnell Douglas and GE, bearing down into the field with their mounted 30 mm Cal M230 Chain Guns and wingtips loaded with HELLFIREs and other firework-named explosives. Do I have to tell you what they were shooting for? Not Yours Truly. Not the boys and girls beside me. So who? Could anyone see anyone? Give me a joke. With the winds kicked up by those bastards' blades like crosses spinning from on high, the winds anyhow, the trash and rubble and dust. Any woman or kid or mankind in cotton and head-dress, any herder, any group carrying a video camera, any box not yet blown to smithereens, they were shooting to shit.

Look, to be young and/or to be kind is to be left open to evil, maybe? Or maybe only if you're partly kind only?

To be evil is to be old and lonesome or should be.

There was once a time when it was all beautiful. Now where is that? I used to hum with love, when I got transcendent or in the right mix.

I walked off toward the mountains, leaving the shooting.

Hubudabis found me and took me farther into the mountains to their caves with rugs and fans and refrigerators run off generators and showed me how to smoke opium, though obvious, it's got great flavor and took the world away as good as pussy ever had. All those old poems about roses just meant pussy and what did they really mean but woman is our great double-sided enthusiasm. That after war or toil, woman is the only respite—and I hope men are so for women but doubt it, and wonder how come? Being a man is tricky, but surely less so than being a woman, I've heard. Being a man now, or a woman now, that's not really the way things are going. It's just about being a person. Sexless. Mainly. And calm.

I decided to get free and start loving. I was going to get clear, aside from the opium scenario. These Hubudabis played great music on record players and they wore cotton and danced with their children. I have always wanted to be everyone else, but have had to be me for so long as to watch others. I'd hope to be evil and done with it all but am afraid of Hell and nurture within me also a great hope for my true heavenly union with Christ and family. This is no joke or hyperholy. I got into dancing and moving around really lightly and in subtle rhythms. There were perfect birds.

Sleeping in caves, I was seeing jungle cats and women with long feet and hairy limbs and I took to dressing only in my knife and long sheep-leather skirt and my hair grew out and I took to the gooch of local girls, whose names I couldn't remember—by gooch I mean roses. Little kisses for rose and rose alike. I walked with a wild man's dance and never switched my clothes. Oh, they thought I was something else. Inside caves the Hubudabis banged on things and made music and burned fires. They loved country music songs from the old gentleman outlaws and I knew every word sometimes and other times made shit up and mumbled. I loved it there with those fine people. Some days or nights the worst fiends in the land came through and played a sort of ball outside on the sand or sat by the fires and drank yak tea. One of the worst had this beautiful overhand spinning serve and he could place that white ball anywhere he pointed his sultanic nose.

The slap of the ball in the sun I enjoyed, and too lusted after their abilities on the court. I played fairly well, sure, but with my vision I often biffed the closest saves.

I got clearer.

Now the yellow men from the East from Asia from who knows where the Hubudabis were not—but were—I felt—beings who trotted out of the first global dawn in Africa. People stepping clean out of the sheer pages of bibles. Curly-headed people—only the evil ones were forcing themselves into the party, as far as I could tell. The good ones paraded around in the sun and floated and swam to the sky.

I got sick off yak milk or gooch—or the opium getting to me at nights. I'd sweat and see the wound inside the world's deep belly. Everything moving each time I opened my eyes, but also a loving community. Deer with blue dots on their foreheads. I only wanted my youth back so I might waste it again—Oh, America, what was Katharine Lee Bates onto anyway?

Where to the gold dream of any fruited plane?

I stepped in one moment to another. I got some goochy and visions. High feelings and plenty wrong with me. I had too much not good inside me, as well as you, maybe do? But listen to this: a good time was had by all. You turn me on? I mean, I had to find pussy, and get all the way into that. It had magic shot through and I was always drawn to the wild show I wasn't supposed to see. The way we talk in the world is gorgeous. I took a long axe and chopped off the arm of the worst fiend at the sticky bone stump while stoned. It was his serving arm. He would never play so beautifully again, nor dance with both arms in the high Arabian style. He would never play between the poles of good and evil with both arms in the fashion most have grown accustomed. It was for those Towers, I'd be happy to say, or for Country. Him speaking graciously of the days of freedom while his men gathered around him at the fire, drinking yak milk and praising terror and all the dark bandits of death and bombings, but I really did it because I was tired of him hotdogging around. He was almost entirely evil—but there was a miserable hope in him—which I likely hacked off or made stronger.

The next thing, I'd feared I'd be AWOL and I went back to base wearing the skirt of sheep and screaming about the heavenly city lost while waving the hacked-off arm around. "I love and hate Indians because I had not the guts they had," I tell the boys. "Still I long for Christ Jesus. I have lost too much of myself to badness I invented or found in myself, but I know what I know and what I believe! I just need more time with family and a better regiment of church and true love. And I finally mean to moan for how I long for Christ," I say. "I had Him and lost Him like a disciple back in that old book, and you are not supposed to do what I have but what can I do but hope he's still with me after all I've done wrong without letting myself be evil, even? What is war? Uplift me Yaoosah!" Where was the arm? Nowhere! Just look at me next to all those men and women. They seemed to understand me, all green and shocked out from war dirty-faced and smoking and plus I lied when I said no one could shoot, they were all sharpshooters covered in death and anxiety. They were tough sons and daughters of bitches and bastards, and I was the fool kid with his heart out.

I guessed they guessed me a freed POW and the Colonel gives me a medal and sends me home with a letter explaining my condition to the general public and health care.

The Letter: Here is our man. H. Roc. We thought he was lost, but he is found. Let him go. Let him come home. He has no idea that he's perfectly stupid. He'll be fine. We'll keep everyone else stop-loss and make them sweat.

The Colonel

She is at the station. Julie, the old bat, her hair a long nest, one tit nosing out. Why, I'm not much better in sheep's leather and my top removed at the station. The buses pull in and idle nowhere. I have a bad banana and America has turned to Shitholeville. Everyone seems flat.

We make it back to the motel where we turn on the calm music. All the way back it was her driving and the sky. Inside our room, the president's a black boob on tv, who shoots people in secret, and I remember sex but it will fail me in the old ways. I don't want to try and make myself try again. Not with her. Not then. I have a cold drink. I taste cinnamon in my coke a cola.

The old California King still lives on, but we've been through the slop, Julie and I. Together and apart I and she have been through the world's puckered-in old butthole. There's a bird that makes a lot of noise out the window. I smell the sea faintly and feel sleepy, and out the window are pastel lights.

I drag Julie into the bath to clean us off from all the fictions. I guide her by her hand into the tub. I begin to fill the dry tub by turning the handle. We stand in the tub in our clothes getting wet. I remove Julie's blouse. I unbutton her buttons. I kiss her belly and her breast and her other breast. We hear the water on our skin. I'd like to say I can fool her and make her feel I care enough, but all she feels is that I care enough to try, even though I can't deliver what she needs, which is nothing, probably, but to get back to her own people wherever her family is, or find a different man.

I wash her. I kneel with her in the waters and I wash her back and shoulders. I get shy and she loves me and hates her man, which is and wasn't me. I wash under her arms. I wash her face, and keep the soap out of her eyes.

I have this and that. I have gotten tired of myself. (You're going to miss me! I swear I'm not coming back for a good while. You're going to miss old Yours Truly out there all alone for a long time. Without Yours Truly with whom to talk.) I have an old RV on the road home, and Julie is hundreds of women that weren't for me, and I was hundreds of men that weren't for her.

I have this and that. A life of highs and lows of mania. Night and fear. A great land that is going away but still has a chance.

APACHE

HALF A HAND was that hand. Three fingers and a crust of dead stump, but what was there, there was plenty for a boy needing to become a man in the West. No, not boy, but the Kid; the real Apache man with the half hand called him Kid, though Kid's name it was not yet. Not earned, and not three fingers but two old fingers and a half thumb was that hand.

The rest missing, the bones cleaved, or fallen off, or what exactly did a Kid say once rattlesnake injected poison so long ago, that the rest of the hand was stolen off the old Apache man forever? What mattered was the desert, the call to count, and above all full lore of the West, Kid might get hold of and keep! If you could mount up and count, if you could beat that Apache who sent the guts out of you, once, you, Kid thought, meaning him, he, might count and have guts once and for the rest of his life might have them, and here he was at a desert ranch, horseracing the man with the half hand halved from rattlesnake hunting barehanded.

Kid was called to ride and count against the old Apache who the Kid called Corporal. All morning Kid had been going wrong. Out for guts with no guts. His horse a thing he forgets and should not forget. His speed, his gripping crop, his wheated mane in the dust. Sun of the desert's red and blonde. Sage, shadow of salt scrub, chaparral—racing through the cholla, saguaro, barrel and yucca and dust. Here in the dust and dirt of kicking deep in a gutless stance high above the arroyos, trying for full gallop to win. Here racing horses that tossed head and snorted in dayheat, Kid kicked and kicked harder to race fastest across the desert sand and stone out in the day's heats. Racing in the arroyos through the chaparral, the Kid on gelding which is the thing he has to have power over, but the gelding is how-many-times bigger than Kid, and the outcroppings, the shadscale, the vastness of the project overtakes his heart. He is to outrace a professional horseman, an Apache weathered hand with a half hand black-heeled and two fingers missing, lost from hunting rattlesnakes at night.

He is not any boy now but is the Kid. The sonofabitch with the hand, the Apache, he named him. His right hand was two thickly calloused fingers and a thumb bitten partly off—this was the right left on him. "A name!" Corporal said the first time they raced, "Can mean everything," if you earn it. "Live for a living." Show yourself to be worthy of naming. "Don't suck hind tit—mother's tit—rich tit."

He can teach the Kid to sing from his guts, the Apache has sworn. To own them and make them work. Pick the rattlers up by hand. The West, the hand, Mother and leaving her forever back by the pool. Mountains to the distance in red and basalt.

There is a church out there. Rattlers to look for tongue breathing. Boots smacked soles first before being put on. A church. A hovel out near the church where the Apache lives alone.

Days ago, the Apache strode up to Mother and said Boss. "Boss, this is the Kid?" Apache had said, and looked Kid in the face, "I hear your brother is dead." Apache stared at Kid and then let his old eyes search to the red hill of the mining mountain, past the iron fence and gate of the pool, beyond ocotillo and mesquite and chaparral saguaro and totem. Past kept grounds to the vast onward expanse.

"Then I'll teach you to race," Apache said after looking more into the Kid's face which didn't move. Mother looked unhappy or unwell. In all the splendor of sun and oddness of saguaro dancing or arms up or multiverticed and coy, the desert alive in winter, the stripped gneiss and red stone and mica in the glare of mindless heat, and every hidden thing the Apache had names for including sidewinder and black rattler and banded Gila.

"Tomorrow after breakfast. Come see." The Apache listened at the Kid's eyes, Kid trying to look back unflinching, un-young, as if worthy of certain particulars—the particulars of which he hadn't had the first thing about knowing.

Paloverde, stucco, ponderosa vegas, lacquered mesquite in herringbone patterned ceilings, this guest-pleasure-ranch Mother owned.

Mother coughed and made a sound low in her pale white underbelly of throat. Neither of the men seemed to notice her. She cleared it away. "Hey there, Cowboy. You better ask my permission. Before wasting your days playing kid stuff with my kid. You work here," she turned up one side of her thin mouth, having bought the ranch and settled into ownership. Being a woman running a dude ranch.

To earn his name Kid had only to steal one race and win it. If he was to count—all he wanted was this—he'd have to earn. All he had to earning his name—to making a name for himself through the gut-flinching races—was the borrowed animal to speak to with his kick. To learn fast to work it around and kick it fast to count. He had been called and named by the great Apache who looked hardly Apache at all, more white and white haired and chord cut in the cheeks, beguiling with strong features of leather so perhaps a bit Apache, his squinting blue eyes, if Kid squinted out in the desert, told to see Apache, told to see Corporal, yes, he saw Apache, plenty of Apache, Hell yes, though he was likely no Corporal to any nation. Yet to say it, that name, to call the man Corporal, did excite certain bodily functions in the Kid, the heart, the eyes, the wetness or dryness of mouth, the desire, fear, the awe and stance, the need for guts-getting.

Made him want to earn his name, have-to-earn-his-goddamn-name-in-the-racing-flats, to see the leathery man with hand on saddle beside him, or not saddled because he was barebacking the buck spine of his Indian pony he rode.

He'd been called. Be this the real desert West or a fake, be him Apache or not full Indian, be him a Corporal or not a real Corporal. Now here were two men, Corporal and Kid, mounted in the furze gold and red of desert, in the chaparral and buckskin, in the sage and death of heat-scented airs in the hot expanse that made him feel unhooked to anything but his need to be called, to change himself, in the desert and close to Mexico, saguaro wide and strange and the fox in their dens and the rattlers asleep, perhaps, near Christmas, but looked for in any chance to pick one up—to see if he would try and pick one up behind the mouth in the months-away-from-flowering hills and be bit if he was to be bit which was the ultimate test and the other truer test, the truest test, was racing full-goddamn-not-flinching speed and winning—beating that tan Apache.

The man raised his half fist into the air and brought it down and they kicked. Kid kicked and kicked again, but the Apache was a black bullet on that black Cayuse with its skew-bald stained white over its rear flank—and he raced Cayuse like a dog, bending its spine, its legs all akick at once. Three horses fast ahead and gaining ground. Kid kicked and jerked within, by the time the Corporal had five lengths ahead or ten—he stopped and hollered, "You lose, Cocksucker. You faking shit," and lit a cigarette and opened a warm Schaefer Light for breakfast. On his horse, smoking and drinking in the sun's morning blinding glare.

"I have foregathered you here for the duty of proving yourself. In proving you care more for yourself than for your very soul," the Apache began, smoke rising. "Your soul, you know, that thing which cannot be proved existent, and that cannot, in truth, be injured. I have brought you here to save you, for you to save yourself, from all that you come from, from your guilt, from shame, *fershtay*? From moral law, from your very home, which was never your home, except by brother, now deceased. Ignis Aurum Probat, gold? Quit fucking losing, Kid."

Upon the flats Kid rode the Apache's other horse. Was big and muscled, fourteen hands at least—twenty-eight of the hand—and they stood, Kid post-defeat, in the desert morning sun, high above the hoof-marked flats. Kid needing to sing from his guts with guts he didn't have and fix land into his dominion—to give a look in the eyes that meant once and always never to lose again, above high ground, ground fast and stomach-flinch inducing in speed across distance. A quail pack ran through. He had lost his only and big brother, was lost himself, and if he lost now he would be forever. There was Mother, too, the only thing he hadn't lost. And Mother was sick, was exactly what he did not want to face, better to prove himself by a man impossible to beat than in her impossible world, where everyone respected her prize which was her money and her act was that of someone who knows they have nothing to fear by nature of their great cash and the great amount of fear they already live with inside themselves. The world was impossible. Death made it. To be with any one and really be with them, before they died, was impossible, and especially not possible was Mother, who showed too much, who owned all, who was sick in her sunchair with swimwear cups too big around her pushed up sunken breasts, showing too much in the sun, holding all. Nearly.

They were mounted. Here was the desert dream. A flat strip to race and test his guts against the man who had them. Apache was seated with his half hand gripping the stiff mane of the small horse, the Cayuse Indian pony he raced, maybe just to prove how weak the Kid was not to win. Apache a smaller man, an old man with bad bones, with pain, with missing bones—with a bit of bone sticking up through the top of his half thumb, sealed in dull clear skin—Corporal was Corporal for having picked up rattlesnakes with the barehand as a boy younger than Kid, and having been struck and bit. Having proved. Having done. Having accomplished what so far Kid had not and must, and if Kid failed he could go back to Mother. Go to where he lunched with her at the pool, and Kid could sulk in faker luxury. Be a shit of her ranch, his brother lost, himself just her boy.

For the rest of his life he could go back to floating and farting around with fakers back at the sun-hot lodge and live there. Because if he could not show his heart and guts and hold his meanness, once—he'd heard every word the Apache Corporal had ever said to him—who was watching him now with those deadblack shaded eyes out of a leather face—then he was a fake Kid at play in a fake dream of a dying West. And he counted for less than desert horseshit pie. If Mother sent him away to school or not. If he got his dick wet ever or not. If he had faith. If he was a sweetheart. If he was anything or not.

"Meanness counts," Apache said.

"Maybe give up, Kid. Go back to the swim pool." He shot Kid a look.

"Maybe quit!"

They had been at this for days.

The air was humid and the sky was changing.

"Know how I lost this hand?" He was going to tell him again. "I cut it off," he said. "With this goddamn filet knife." He patted his side where the knife hugged in its sheath with bone sticking out for handle.

"I know it. And I will beat you."

"One day isn't enough! I can't wait. I won't. I don't want you to learn. I want you to have. To steal it. A posteriori, Cunt!"

Not that the pool was laid without any promise. But he could not go back anyhow to the pool and live with fakers, because should he lose and go back to the lodge he would know his failure and the girl, the redhead he told his dream of beating the Apache, would know and Mother would.

At the pool there were girls and women with wet swimwear ties soaking through places in wraps and pullovers, wet and held against the naked sun-hot flesh. The redheaded girl he'd been with in the flats one night. And another night. Last night! There were drinks at the pool and getups and memories in other families and the plates of food and girls' magazines and a world he wanted nothing to do with that Mother owned.

Then there was Mother, who he was afraid he cared too much for, even after how she treated Brother, to give himself over to meanness and true hatred.

There was Brother, gone. It made Kid mad to think of him. Drinking, slapping a man over their seats at a singing man's show, riding his motorcycle alone, smiling his smile from boyhood, a guy who was how he was, hardly a distance from himself and himself, there in front of you, knowing he was every inch, not putting on a show, laughing, owning a pistol he drove with, a giant with a laugh like a holiday, two hundred and forty pounds of him without fear, his pockets full of used tissues and mints and always a pack of cigarettes, and his stash, the giant heart in him on the road, but not on the road, but dead. A brother is not a thing to live after without, all of him that was charging into the heart of the country to experience what was happening inside, calmly, centered, profoundly deep, holding it all to himself except the great love he sent right out to anyone worthy.

Mother had bought the resort ranch and their dad was left by Mother and Brother was dead. Brother was nothing like girl assing at the pool. Nothing like Mother. Nothing like any of this, but most like the Apache, but not like Apache.

Staring at the hand made him feel meanness, hatred, his own will. The Corporal who cut one hand half off with another to survive snakebite. Slicing a line from the wedge between middle and ring finger and cutting down to the cuff of wrist. A cuff of wrist and black handcrust remained above the greasecloth sleeve. No ring on either half hand or full hand.

The Apache stared and started up again, sky darkening. "You farting sack of piss." He stared at the Kid. "Fart piss. Pee bubble."

"How are you to ride with me with guts without your guts?" he said. "Who besides me can teach you? Who cares what hurts you? Who cares what you feel! You have to hate the whole world. You have to hate what's not yours. Then you'll love. Maybe quit! You don't have it. Go back to the pool and feel kind of sexy and girl-like digging your crotch into the chair and look out at twat. Give up. Find pussy, maybe. Instead of all of this." He gestured to his wide homeland. "Forget redemption. What are you doing out here anyway. You have heart, but it won't work for its glory."

Kid *had* lain in a sunchair and done just that. He'd felt rather girl-like doing just those things, and liked pretty well the feeling. Despite his riding morning and post-lunch, despite lifting weights, pumping iron until his vision turned purple and gold, he lay there feeling sore and sexy at the pool, feeling thin and warm, his chin on cupped hands, butt arched up to the sky, digesting alongside Mother at lunch, eking out a little gas here and there, back where you had to hide your farts, because hiding gas and faking around was all under all that sun.

The Apache lived out in the desert.

Without girls who'd shaved themselves or God-knows to wear what they had on at the ranch. In a squat with a retard and the A/C—A/C he said he bought her at Younkers Department Store. Because he loved her and she wanted it.

A real retarded woman kept in the desert scrub and sand, at his squat, the Corporal's. Corporal so old and leathered.

The Kid hated him. As much as he'd told Kid to hate him. No more. Hated Mother. Barely. Hated pool. Younkers Department Store and the A/C? Retard? Brother would laugh. He'd fall apart laughing. This fake shit, he'd call it. This bullshit Apache! *Horizontal Retard*, the Corporal called her, waiting on him back for him after he rode and won. Brother who had the same face as Kid would laugh. The same voice Kid had stolen long ago, had copied, but couldn't get the heart.

Where was Brother now—out in the gold, up in the wind, up in the high windblown dust, up in the hawk and swoop? The high yonder? Not enough. High heaven? Fuck it.

The whole earth was done. A little shade here. Birds. Trailers with toilets that ran in long pipes through the desert to spill into sand, and chevron TV antennas and running water and no septic. A retard in lace chiffon smoking cigarettes. Or was there a retard? Was it all lies? The stories of the Apaches riding half-off-horseside saddleless and shooting arrows, destroying their enemies, then run off cliffs to death in Texas by half-ass whites with no honor, all the West, only to work for Mother? Fort Davis? The Mescalero Apaches Apache told Kid about? Geronimo and Dahteste—the fighting woman? All in the span of human time on earth, a moment in light of the billions of years of light on this earth.

Before them, the sea had been over this land. Had Kid enough time to study the seabed and live out the desert long enough alongside Apache, discovering the history of arrowheads and fossils found in the earth, the change of millions of years, *billions*!—each gas and element made mineral turned plant, turned finger grown from sidefin, the redhead and Kid and Apache, if allowed time. But there was never enough time before the Apache wanted to see some show. Some heart. Will.

Lies or not, fart pie to retards and Mother! To himgoddamnself. To losing to any man on any fucking pony.

The man held his half hand up to the sky. Held it high, two fingers and half thumb, like a wild-ass Christ, and when they came down they would kick hard. Kid's stomach charged before the hand came down, forgetting the horse, forgetting blood. Forgetting he had only one thing to count with, that horse to race with all his have-to-have-it or go mad with self-will, but they didn't race. They didn't ride.

A first rain fell hard. Apache looked over at Kid.

"Look at me now, my Kid."

The Kid looked back at the man's eyes. American Rock and Roll and the brother Kid was thinking of in the first rain he'd ever felt in a desert. Their father's music that became theirs. The first guitar chords, the feedback, then the drums coming in like a heart pumping above the real heart, faking almost at first, but building, knowing in blood that what was coming was right and the chords building and repeating, pumping harder, grown into rockets that lifted off and ripped into strange spheres, leaving the world behind. His father who'd been a GOD to Kid, terrified him, then grew out of it.... Rain fell and the man was staring into him—Kid feeling the guitars pulling his veins off their courses, redirecting blood as the buildings fell and the explosions tore the world down. The saguaros stood and drums pumped blood out from where explosions had opened inside—in the great desert the body became wounded and was leaking, drums beating blood into the sand. Brother loved this. He had lived this way and left, in rock and roll, in knowing himself, in altered pain—in the final release of putting it all on the line and throwing up his huge hands.

"You don't have it. Not today," Apache said. "You will have it, by Christ. But I won't hold my breath. You better find it. Fend for yourself. I'm going to blow off some spunk with my retard. She gives all of herself—every time. Not like you, who doesn't give shit. You faking fart."

Kid knew talk from talk. He was feeling ready and would be more so when the day cleared and the clouds let go of the last rains. He felt himself in his body, good or bad, real or not real, ready to give all whether he deserved to or didn't deserve. He would. He'd race this afternoon and take it. But was what the man just said about Kid true? Could he have it? Could he practice to earn it? No. He had to have it right then, Apache said, matter now or fail. Count or be nothing.

The man was no Corporal, and most of what he said most often must be a lie. Still, the Apache was the fastest man at the ranch. The toughest. The little mean old shit, with the inspired face. He could speak with his bloodspeak to the Cayuse, to any horse, and didn't need words or even to kick.

In the sagging V of the man's oilcloth shirt, a small lump of something stuck to a hair, a single white chest hair. What was it? A chink of soap? The A/C had hardened it in the cold air on the hair? The Apache saw Kid staring and down. He pulled it off, in the rain, and rubbed it between his first two fingers and half of thumb. Made an old face, the old god. Soap? Spunk? As of when did he have a chink of anygoddamnthing stuck to him, the Apache's face seemed to ask? Never. Never did he have one lump of any chink of nothing stuck to any hair. It was too cold in the place? It was the retard's A/C?

"Let's go." He chatted the Cayuse and Kid got his horse turned around and leading and fought to keep him from running back to the corral and they rode in in the hot rain. The

Apache would head back in his rig to his squat. From the rain would come blanket flowers, Mexican poppies orange across the hills, hibiscus, lupine, wild onion, owl's clover—names of flowers Apache had said over again, pointing to the dry dead earth on their first rides, blue fiesta, brittlebush, creosote flower, signaling what would go where, as if by the magic of names he could summon colors from the earth's palette covering the land of dry dust, horses from his very heart, women from his very loins, bones from his bad hand, life from life, simply by naming, so great were his stocks in the whole thing.

Kid passed the gardens on the path to his room at the ranch. His suite. The day was a bust. Back by the buck and barrel and beavertail alongside the path, he kicked a clod with the toe of a boot and scattered it across the cement, dirt over the walkway the workers would have to clean when the rain stopped. Mexicanos. Mother's. Her workers. She owned the guest ranch. He thought of the man and his retard.

Hell of an idea was that retard. A show of a concept. Was that all he could get? Were they better in the sack? The Apache had stolen her, he'd said, from the only friend he had had, up in Colorado. The man who claimed himself real live Apache. Who'd lived everywhere. Lived in New York City and had a top office, somehow, wearing his hat, stiff greasecloth and feathers—lived in California in blue jeans, was in films, had bush galore, and was living now in a squat in Arizona near Mexico with a retard in A/C—and would soon be blowing his spunk, old man, in the A/C? Was this anywise the West?

Kid thought of his redhaired girl who just last night he was with in the purple flats beside a small fire he had made, the girl and her slick running shorts and thin shirt, her music of her blood he could sense, the southerly desert moon, the chill and hot rush of feeling inside her, in her running shorts, up high a little, higher inside, and her saying wait in a way he felt she too felt it, his desire bigger than that animal he rode, all that fear, all that glory. She felt it too but said wait...why, he couldn't know. Kid had waited. Then yes she whispered, "Let's go for it," in the night flats, in the dust. What made her want Kid, he didn't know, but he wanted it all, the full holy and perverse merging, switching places and joining, the wild rush of heat and cool air, escaping everything wrong in favor of everything right in wrongness, beyond the world of their world, into the physical heat and new vision by fire.

Old Apache was going to blow his spunk? How ridiculous. In the A/C no less? Kid was not going to be in any A/C nor going to blow his spunk either. He wasn't fooling around. He was going to stay out of air-conditioning altogether and lift in the gym and be ready. He fit his key in the door and had an idea and certainly wasn't about to blow any spunk or sit in A/C breathing that A/C smell in the rain. He was going to get the jump on that Apache. He would get it following a plan he came up with in the rain before and while kicking the dirt clod, and fastening the plan as he stepped on the heel of his boot with his boot and pried his foot out.

He would be working out, pronto, not in the A/C. While keeping his spunk. This was getting a jump. He stood on the other heel with his socked foot and tried to wiggle his foot free and fell on the sofa. How ludicrous. How flopping and stupid and fake. This suite. This was not getting a jump. This was no jumping. The A/C came on. Not that he had asked for it.

He took off his jeans while sitting on the tacked cowhide sofa. He felt girlish doing it like this, looking at himself in undies. All that cow under him. So he stood up. He got them off. This was getting more like it. He went into the bathroom where the air was on. He put on his gym shorts and shirt. He had no hair buzzing any places. He looked at himself like a man about to get the jump on another man. Especially when that other man is a real old Apache with one hand half missing, and he considered his plan.

He checked it over with Brother in his heart.

He survived by keeping his brother in his heart to talk to. Nights Brother came to see him in his dreams and they both knew it wasn't true and he was still alive and they talked about it. Lately, he could tell in dreams that he knew better than to believe anyone was really there. He could see every detail of his face, hear him talk, grab hold of him. Days, Kid talked to him and believed Brother could hear his thoughts and see him, and it was going away. Even this was fading. It wasn't the best plan, but he could sense his need, surely. The Apache would see it as genius or see it as cowardlysome—but he would see. He had told Kid what Kid had to do, to take it no matter what. He would try to get it right. To not ruin anything—just to get the jump. Just to goddamn count.

Kid laced up his workout shoes and looked at himself. He did and didn't look like a man who had, but he saw in his eyes the look of one who knew how important it was to have it. To push one's self to take or push one's self to take but keep trying and never give one's self the permission—this was it. He either had to give it to himself. Permission right then. Or not.

He stepped outside, Jesus, Fuck, and there was Mother.

"Sonofabitch," he said. There was the girl with her. The only girl, beside and a bit behind Mother. "Shit."

They both stood there gawking at Kid, sun all over the wet place.

"Is that how you mightn't greet your mother?" Mother pretended to scold. Then she looked genuinely hurt. Then lost. Fuck. He didn't need anyone's permission. He loved her. He hated her. He loved and hated everyone. What was the redhead doing? Mother was wearing peach and looking old. She looked old and in peach and her hair was effervescent and cut short in a bowlish expensive cut.

Brother had been her first child and once she'd been a good mom. He felt loyalty to Brother who would not speak with her before he was gone. Now there was the redhead standing beside her, a bit behind, and all of it a trap.

"Look, I met a new friend today." Mother held up her arms a bit, showing the strange silk shirt with big sleeves she wore after the rain. Peach. She said friend like maybe she was aware of the falseness of calling any girl a friend, especially one who would associate with her kid. All of this, seemed to Kid, was in how she said it. "Says you two already know one another! How about lunch." Mother grimaced. Surely Mother was joking? She meant to smile? Was Kid so bad as to make a mother set on smiling grimace? When she means to only smile at her kid? Nothing says Kid. Fart pie, he wants to say. Fuck soup. "Okie Doke," he finally says. "Let me put riding clothes back on."

He looked at Mother, who smiled only with the muscles in her mouth and jaw.

He looked at the redhaired girl from the night, in running shorts, smiling in sun.

How did Mother get her involved with Mother? "Think the rain is done?" he said to the girl, fake smiling. "Oh Brother."

He went to his room. In the room the air was going nuts. Back outside, she had the poor girl's ear. They were off to eat soup. Mother had won. Mother was smiling and talking quietly to the girl.

They ate. They sat. The Kid was Kid. Sun was out. He stared off to the red mountain where the Apache lived and with the huge sky above. Needless to say where he must be in the A/C. Out to where he was unsuspecting, surely, blowing out his spunk? No idea that things would be different this one time, after lunch, this day. Mother and the girl talked, the girl glancing at him, picking at this and that, chewing. Mother smiled and showed the world she still had it, was still a beauty, was capable of facing the world and playing her part. Even after the family funeral. Even…after all the years in the late Earth and her life mostly used up in children—still searching to show herself. To prove she had it—and to prove she had she had this ranch. One place where the rich came to ride and soak and live it up in the gold and red of desert. Crystal on the table. Good silver. Bamboo cloths. Mexicans wearing string bowties holding silver pitchers of hibiscus tea floating great cubes of ice on top and all this sun. Lately, she'd been putting up signs all around on posts.

Fake pressed wood-board and lacquered signs that read: *Do Not Block Roadway. No Parking.* Worse still: *NO PORKING* with a wild boar, which weren't even in this part of the desert. *SNAKE CROSSING*, with a picture of one snake mounted by another, drawn with big faking rattles, the two approached like dogs, a crudely drawn snake penis launched out of the "male" snake's underbelly, grins on their snake faces. It was pathetic! The sex organs were internal on snakes and everybody knew. There was an illness of trouble and sadness after each thing she did that arrived in her face but which she tried to hide. Kid stared off at the mountain. The girl looked at him, trying to get Kid to knock it off. He had been in his body, he was thinking, and it didn't matter, and now it all was to be different. With a difference he announced he was off to race and beat that sonofabitch Apache!

"I'm going to go beat that goddamn Apache."

Mother knew how to stop him, and how to keep him at the table.

"He's not real Apache," said Mother. "Not a true one, no. Puerto Rican. Or Peruvian maybe, a 20th of either. Or just worn down saddle wet and drunk," she said. "A hundred dollars says he's no amount real Apache." She put both hands flat on the table. She stood. Reached out her hand to Kid.

"Bet me. Two hundred."

She looked between the boy's eyes. Her son's, before the girl he liked and who liked her boy.

She wanted to bet on something that could not be proved but by the Apache, and that was going to cost a lot more than a few hundred dollars. That would cost the entire game, all of his life, and even then it could not be bought, the proof.

"Come on, bet me."

She was standing, hand out, open and turned upward in the sun. "Probably caught his hand in a garbage disposal. I know someone that happened to."

She was louder.

"The wife turned it on with his hand down inside. You laugh?" No one had. "Spend the afternoon with us. It's almost Christmas." She lowered her eyes. She lifted her hands up to appraise the place she owns all of. She looked around and smiled. Guests looked. Her hair was thin and colored in an expensive show of blonde. "This isn't the real West, Son," she pretend laughed. "This isn't that real. Don't you know what a night here costs?" She brought down her hands. She looked sad for him and old. "It is a pleasure ranch. It's all for pleasure." She stood looking at him like she could not believe him. "Five hundred dollars a night. And that's just for the bed and coffee. Add riding. Add golf. Add massage, facials, kid camp, room service, cocktails, Son. The whole thing. Add tax. Add state and federal, Kiddo. Add inflation. Plus tip. Figure in the sleeves of balls. The suntan oil, and the shops! Don't forget who owns this place. Don't forget who is no fool. This isn't cowboys and Indians! This isn't about Goddamned Indians!"

"I'm going to race," Kid said and stood and got away from the table. He strode toward the corral, leaving Mother's table behind him. And the girl. Away from all the pleasure.

The plan was to kick the Apache man's horse in the face with his right spur. He did it.

As soon as they'd reached the flats, the hand rose up in the air, the spunk blown or not, the retard retarded or not and the hand came down, Kid remembered his horse. He got just enough ahead with his foot out of stirrup, and kicked the spur back into the eye. Hit the face with the spur, hard, and felt it connect. The Cayuse threw and rolled and bled. It was awful to hear the sound. The small man was fast under the small horse with his old leg under; he looked bigger with the downed horse. The horse was rubbing him into the rocks. The eye of the Cayuse was bloody and bubbled. Apache groaned and seemed to be having an attack in his mind. He didn't look right, with the jerking and the spittle. The man gripped his hand into a crack in a great flat rock, like an altar he was pinned to, and he shook. Cried out nonsense in his terrible shaking and it was so real in the earth seeing the man like that. A small rattler from the handhold bit him. Christ. There it was in the air ahold of that halved hand and Kid grabbed the filet knife off him. He cut the snake, small thing, baby, no control over its poison, getting his own shirt off, and cutting it into a tourniquet that he wound so tight under the wrist and tied it. With the filet knife, Kid pierced into the man's wrist center and cut, the rest of the man's hand, off, which was tough to do, going between bone and joint and getting through skin and strings. Apache screamed and cried out, even in his terrible shaking fit, and Kid had to pop the joint out and slice through skin. The screaming. The vastness of sound and wetness and soundlessness. This is what the Apache had done long ago, cutting off the poison, but was that right?

In the sand it lay there. A thing Kid didn't want to look at and was trying to forget while seeing it. In stillness, as if not there, ripe, vacant, loud in its deadness with the black parts dead from long before—and then it was time to move—God—fast.

He grabbed the man and pulled him, helped him to saddle the horse. Kid rode him in to the corral on the front of the Kid's horse. At the corral he got someone to drive them to the hospital in town. He'd kicked the pony's eye and left it writhing there in the dust. He'd gotten the Apache to help. Left the crazed Cayuse writhing with the torn eye by the hand.

The man was released back to the ranch, and days after Kid finally rode out to see him at his trailer and squat. The old man was angry. About his horse. Hand. Heart attack. Bum leg.

Plenty of things he was angry about. He was older looking than he had been on horseback days in his hat and oilcloth. There were patches of pink that showed on his old whiskered neck and on his face and hands. Still, he was proud and stubborn. Kid had never been out to see the old man's home, leather tack and old plywood were littered around the trailer. Fenders in the sand in the white pipe-fenced yardless yard.

While drinking, the old man was silent. He would glare at him sometimes. But what could be said? He tossed him a first beer, after some time making him sit in the silence of the not far away dusk, and they drank in the small heat of a golden-lit world different than days past. They didn't belong anywhere, and they didn't belong together. Certainly weren't friends—weren't going to head in and sit by the pool at Mother's resort, the two of them, men and women nearby with drinks and magazines.

So this was that.

"I know what I know, and I know what you don't," the man said. "I know you don't know shit. I know in my blood what I got and I know what you got and what you don't. Kicking a horse's eye. You puny shit coward. You left my horse to suffer."

The two sat under the antennae that rose above the Apache's trailer, looking out at nothing. Apache drinking from his left hand in the brightening blue of the mountains, blanket flower beyond, and night coming with the cool coming down. At the old trailer with the waste tube running out to the desert, how many retards could be found? How many other people? How much new A/C? From Younkers or Sears or elsewhere? They were the two of them—a young man and old man—and nothing to prove remained. The man had had a real heart attack.

"What you do have is need," the old man concluded. "But who are you, Kid? Without me, or your mom, or brother?"

Mother had heard the man's horse had been blinded, and the men had gone out and put it down—even the Cayuse, it turned out, she had owned. She knew about the hand. There was something good with her, too, and she found her way the best she could, and kept up her part of the act. She could keep rising up better than before. She kept herself up. He knew death and races in the desert and fear and how to overcome some of it—but he wondered if he were a fraud—he hadn't proved himself without cheating.

He had done and he'd seen the truth—ah, madness and lies and human farce and kindness—and now he needed to hide it from himself. He could not let himself get closer to people—he had always been far away from himself and right there pushing to have each moment deliver itself like God rising from the desert in gold and music and covered in penises, redheads, and virgins riding upon Him—the great aggregate whole receding with each approach. He wanted back in that riding and needing with all his heart, wanting, and needing, having to have then what the Apache had, and thinking it could be done; that old sonofabitch—the boy thinking he could win that sort of thing—true greatness of will. Wanting to prove. He had killed the Cayuse. Almost murdered the Apache.

What right did a guy have?

Slaughter the horses.

He would see his brother in heaven or there was no such thing—if not—if so, then this was the horridedessly beautiful thing here on the world. Even a fool or a coward can see it and feel it—that *if* there's nothing more than this life it is the wildest and most painful farce. The art of being here to watch the ones you love go away from you, and die—and one's self slip away. If there's more, why can't we know? Why stay, if we are to be cowards, most of all? All except the Apache, who lost none of himself in anyone's eyes or by any sense perceivable except by that hand, now gone.

A hundred hands a hundred times cut them off him. Leave the hero deformed. A great resounding love to the deformed man, and our sorrow, and our admirations.

The Apache had given him a call, a symbol of the life—the old Native. Native? No. Call him original, a self-fashioned old kind, self-formed and devoted to himself, his vanity, his craft, his skill, and performance—his greatness of difference in performance most of all, his absolute devotion to his performance.

For a kid's sake the brother should have lived, but didn't. The Apache looked at the boy. "Stop feeling sorry for yourself. I lost my hand, and you know what, I'm going to get pussy. Good rich pussy. With only one hand, with all the will left in me, I'll excite the waters. That which is more in me than you'll ever have. In each of the fingers of this full hand." He held up the hand and he still had it, in the eyes, the wild firing charm of confidence. "Even in the pinky! More pussy than you'll ever know. Is what I have ahead of me."

Apache, the thunderhead, the human god let him live forever, the most genius—the imbecile—the boy was done feeling shame. But the Apache had stories similar to tell, family lost, life maddened, head yet alert—wildly watching and alive before his eyes—decided on the adventure of having a hot heart, for or against each person entirely. That goddamned old man had his, he, himself's, the young man's love, all of it, for he had given the boy something. Everything. It still couldn't be enough. The young man would decide for himself. The odds. A fully galloped race counted only. Half of a hand now none. You have to stay in the race to win, even when no one wins. Your brother is your brother. A star appeared. Lightning on the distant shore over the mountains.

They sat and watched it come and saw it to dark.

In their time, two by two, the boy would only change one thing and that he could never change. Then there was the time with the Apache. They had had some rides.

HOGS

ONE WENT FOR TWO and became one again. I'm telling you of me and my mother. Meaning a boy beside his mother, and the mother sleeping. Two was just one confusing itself. A person could get sick like this, to put a fine point on the end of things.

There was a little house in the yard behind the house. Can you imagine? The possibilities in the mind, when there was more than one house? A house behind a house, like for kids? Like for a boy. Another world beyond the world!

There was corn out one window and over the other window was a sheet. Here was summer to wake up wild. Here, a summer to chase chickens. And the hot hogs that squealed in the hog stalls next door. His mother lay sleeping. His brother was not there and his sister was not there. Only he.

Her hand held long bones and the ropes rolled and

popped under her skin. She let him work the ropes back and forth across her bones, but one could get bored with it. The selfish self not getting any response. It was only her loose skin that he knew. And what lay underneath there? It was harder.

And what lay underneath that hardness? A mother? On a morning. Still sleeping.

Light came cauliflower across the sheets, then mushroom, then cauliflower again. The light almost touched one's hair. It was the kind of light you wanted more and more of. It would not reach her face. He touched her hair. Morning doves cooed wooden sounds in the corn. The sheets were hung. You could get sick. A person.

There was a closet with old things inside—baby clothes, a chest. Wedding gowns. This was the room his mother had grown up in. And then other sisters had taken over the room for a turn. In the closet, also, were trophies. Other dresses.

Up close her face looked made in light. The closet smelled like wood and dust. A small bird and its shadow flew across the sheet over the window. Strings on her bones popped in and out of place. Places, places, houses! Imagine. The shadow was gone. The bird was gone. It was already late in summer.

The closet held old trophies she had won.

She had run so fast.

Scraps of paper cut from papers said so.

She was tired, tired—she had run.

With her face near, he felt air come out. Slipping lower, he ran his leg down one of her legs. He felt her smoothness and then her short leg hairs tugged.

Sleep, she said.

Her mouth was shut. He heard a tractor. He imagined little bits of husk floating. She breathed through her nose.

There was the little house behind the house where he could go!

The tractor hummed. Birds. There were the hogs squealing at the hog farm. He placed his head on his fist, his elbow went into the mattress and he looked at her good. There was so much time to one day, one morning. A life. Her mouth was dead closed and she breathed in her throat like little pigs talking in the air. He looked at her hair.

OUT THERE

OUT THERE (out there, out there, out there—I am going to level with you. Worst story in the book is this story in the book. So I am going to spruce it out, spur it up, add some kitchen spice. Hey, I'm back. The spice is in the RV here, at my table, in the motor coach, overlooking the old Cliff House in San Francisco at Land's End. Here's a tip: San Francisco is over. There's a moratorium on the old hunting grounds. There isn't lunatic delight or rose heaven or anything left here up north of LA. Nights ago, I was at the Malibu Beach RV Park after six days of going nuts inside Los Angeles, wrecking a Japanese car with my 31-footer, losing my status as the great conductor of the West, of my time, of my mind, chasing girls, meeting some first class women and one in particular, a great artist, no Catherine, but Irish, at least, and she and I were at the RV Park in Malibu after no sleep for days running around LA and staying with the Motor Coach parked in her gated community next to so-and-so famous lady actor's house and parked at the park overlooking the great sea below crashing full of breakers, naked in the Coach smoking, listening to the old soft music of the songwriters singing of this great country and its impossibility of being understood, being held, all of it escaping the grasp, too far to reach, and having reached the sea, the whole sea crashing and no more land, the end of a great and mighty journey in an unsafe, definitely unsafe rig, wheeling around half cocked wild and manic and pissing off everyone in sight, under the police radar, a great airplane coach on the road with no insurance, no license to be as nuts as I am, her and I nude smoking and seeing that sea—out there—the madness in me—and in her—the inevitable end of journey, a moment to rest and sleep like a child overlooking the slamming of sea—you know—to feel, before sleep, the listening, to listen, listen—and see and feel what is lost and cannot be regained, what has escaped the grasp, what every journey feels at the end of a long wild stretch where nothing is held and all is lost and fantastical. America still exists when you do it all wrong and wild and mad and manic in a big long probably unsafe, absolutely unsafe, American automobile home scamp pad Bounder whale yacht—shocks blown—bushings bushed—one wheel on the left rear in the two hollow without air—if the other blows: explosion city—flip city—death trap—and the next day I spent the day tearing my hands apart in Oxnard, California, with a pack of Mexican guys in an old gravel lot beside the Oxnard Airport beside the animal shelter with the dogs going nuts in agony in the heat and abandonment and captivity in their wild hearts—*out there*—learning to fix lights and fiberglass and tires on old Bounder, the MC, Motor Coach, the thing my brother bought me, ((without knowing he bought me)), to see our great nation. While fixing the Bounder ((turns out I didn't fix it because I am here in SF with air leaking from the tire on the back left, chasing auto-part-store personnel and Firestone Tire Co. employees like a madman shouting and taking off the hubcaps, frinking with the screws and after taking the screws out by chiseling notches into the heads to hammer and chisel these from their grooves, and getting lug nut covers off, then on foot chasing a size 38 (1 and ½ inch) socket at the auto parts stores up and down Geary because the good old mechanics in this town are children, because there is a moratorium on anything real in this city: real mechanics, real wildmen, real girls, real anything—plus my lug nuts are commercial and I'm off the semi-trucking routes, here on Geary—and I'll tell you what I saw above Malibu, people they call lunatics and hippies and "out there" people, doing nothing, camping on the beach, on the shittiest beaches, above the sun, up before Ventura, Scuzz Beach, *Thornhill Broom Beach*, doing nothing, just sitting there in little shit motor coaches, short little rigs, lying on their backs on pool chairs, and then here, SF, and coaches all down Fulton, coaches galore, all mildewed and needle coated, spray painted, graffitied, destitute, this town asleep, or dead, nothing how I left it so many years ago, nothing like when my teacher got here, even more years ago—when it was city and sun and kid delight, us all free, and both sexes, all sexes, delighting in tomfoolery and the sky ceilingless and Jupiter-like and pre-New World, us all kids from childhood city being kids as adults, and me fixing the coach)), Coach calls, old teacher, while I'm tearing up my hands in the sun, my dog run off, my teacher phoning, and I answer and tell him I'm *out there* in a 31-foot coach and my dog Jewely has run off and that's *Oxnard Airport* in a field with Mexican guys and me tearing my hands apart like a nut. *Out there*, I tell you. I tell him. He laughs. When he does it he says, *Ha.* He wants me to send him a personal hygiene product, Look, marital aid, he instructs. He can't find it. In all of old NY. Our running prank. Me buying it for him. It's his way of telling me he is out of the stuff he needs but not out of his real stuff he needs for the fucking. This select product is appreciably better, as he has explained to me, than all the other near infinitudes of selectables from its category. This is to say, he knows one thing from another—and this one from all the others, the others he doesn't like nearly so much as this brand. Is this to say, he wants to impress me with what he knows or to impress upon me that I am beneath myself buying an old guy his marital aids? This is to say, he is a connoisseur of this field and that variety amidst the folderol of unoffending-looking other products in the category of the shelf facings of this category—is best? Saying he still has the fucking down as far as the being able, and he still has the itch to go out there going up and up and up—none of which matters, in the talking, except two guys trying to push each other to keep the game going, which is stupid. He is going in for surgery, he finally gets clear and simple. He sounds nervous. He's never told me about anything like this, but I've heard about this from others. He has got bad health going with his health. Doctors! I think of him, and I think of me, in Oxnard, secretly happy as hell to be me laboring at the task, with the Mexicans, hands covered black in grease and with them smoking and spitting and speaking Spanish and working on the rig in the hot sun for six hours, their tools all a mess, fixing what hell I tore up on the coach hitting that other car, having driven like a nut all over LA in a 31-foot plane, meeting girls, Jewely getting everyone's attention, her blue eye with the star in it, the mandala around the eyeball, her genius looks and pure spirit, from heaven, us chasing tail, dealing with cops, pistol in the back bedroom, bullets, the big radio and a lot of highway behind, a lot of grainy nights, pitch black with moon and stars and rock and roll, old tucked away DJs and radio shows of lost America through the open nothing nights, charging onward...feeling that my teacher wishes he were out in freedom and not facing the knife—him who is always with me at the wheel and sometimes the keys, and I said, I'm with you, always, Coach, *green bananas and tiger milk*—I told him from Oxnard—*Hugs and Kisses* as he always signed off—the wild famous genius who saved fiction—and I thought of him as I drove up the 101 with the purple mountains in the post-dusk falling night.... He was the one I called when I lost my brother. Listen, Listen, dammit, should you want to know the truth. I feel lousy as hell about chasing girls and talking the way I talk. You want to know the truth? As one man to whoever, I feel compelled, urged, to show off. Talking about roses and girls. These lunatic stories. Give me a break. What a joke. Pussy heaven. Ha. The world won't want to hear this shit out of me, but the truth is I feel lousy. Those dogs howling in their kennels. The whole world aching to come back to life from the life we are all in up to up to our eyeballs. Everyone splintered over this and that word because they can't change a light bulb in terms of getting a new joke together. I feel bad to God, when the truth is said, God's honest truth: I want to be there for the world and for the people I love and for the people I don't even love. All this talk about nishy is just, for me anyhow, just talk—unless I can find someone to spend some time with and then you know...make things better. But really I am thinking about my teacher, and worrying for him, though I know he will live on, I am sure, unkillable as he is, but then I have been wrong.

He is with me, them both, as men, Carl and Coach, Catherine is not with me as she could be, though she calls from time to time—informs me I can propose in eight more years, tells me this and that, does she still love me, because I won't quit, because my teacher wants to pay me for the marital product for his girlfriend and his use, because I said, *Hey, Pal, this one is on me...overnight shipped to your door, you know*...since...*I just don't want anyone to get hurt*, and he laughed, and he said that's funny—*Ha*—then he calls me as I am in SF and I say *moratorium*, and he threatens to call my parents and the police if I won't give him my address to pay me back, and I say I don't give a damn about the constabulary forces, and he's been through the knife and he's fine—I say I will trade the juice for this and that word, for this and that totem, because I want to tell him about the Eagle Feather and he says let me read this book if I want his this word and that word for the book, and I say I don't want anyone to read this book, just write the following and told him what I wanted him to write—which do I even have to tell you he refused; told him I just want to be on the next tear and the next, chasing that which cannot be held, to the sea and spume and spunk, to the city, to what is out there...too many goddamned people you care about...and the one that isn't here... all of it in here and *out there* ((P.S. Don't come to SF! Learn to work on a rig. Learn to take out stripped screws with a chisel and a hammer, learn to run on gas, learn to have your piss the color of egg yellows and smelling like gasoline or diesel, learn to conduct a wild machine through tight conditions, to get delusional enough to never stop, to be up up up, for the people who need you, because you need them, because it's about what kind of a story you can make for yourself so while driving it's you and big Carl, and you and the teacher, and still burning for Catherine, and Jewely eating a dry rabbit that looks like a muff—the humor of that—a big dry bunny merkin—and the girl in this story you have to sacrifice, you have to take advantage of, you have to push on beyond, girl or boy, you or them, if it is not true love, because you have to be shaking rattling and rolling through cities in search of what's out ahead, manic, trying to take care of everyone, though you didn't save your own, though you failed, can't go back, dreaming up moves to write, San Francisco, what a letdown! Oregon up ahead! No place to stop but to stop in and see your great sister, the one who keeps you alive, you two go sit together both of you feeling together what it is to have lost, both, your shared brother, the kid sister who is the only one you let run your ship this way or that way, your sister the artist, your great family, you in a coach with no money and no fame and so it's onward, never stopping, never dying, scribbling the adventure in your head which is always better in life than on paper, getting yourself big and ready, being a real man, or woman, a real nut, making something to last a little longer than yourself, your moods, your age, your teaching class, and when I came to SF and it's dead city. So here is the end of one journey, and it's time to move on, time to find the next great disaster, the old teacher with me always, as he was with the great so-and-so and the other great so-and-so except of course not, as I am like the child and he is like the Coach, and they were women and men to men and would have told him *fuck off Coach and buy your own lube!*, and New York is where you want to be, LA is where you want to be, up and at it, in the sun action, or in the weather action, trying to make something out of yourself, trying to figure out how to present yourself as yourself, making up your myth, finding a way in.... Fuck San Francisco, Fuck all except having something funny to tell, so that when your brother calls, you don't let him down, because you let him down, and tonight the great jumping bean I know, one of the greatest, will land in Oakland, and we will launch for the north, still with the back tire leaking air out of the valve that cannot be tightened, and if it blows we go side over and full of 60 gallons of gas and twenty of propane, rolling further up and *out there*, up the winding logging road to Eureka, driving like a Wildman, flying the curves at 80, 85, hair-pinners, wherever it goes, after the end of this journey, in the old city, overlooking the Cliff House, overlooking Land's End...)) and so here it is, that lousy story). *Out There* beyond the tables, past the candles and the bar and the chairs and stations, over all the seats with the couples having dinner, over the head of the daughter of J.P.B., his name not stated to protect the person he is—she who works at a bar and restaurant on First in NY where they actually serve a cocktail called the Vision Cleanse, which really is a cleanse, cayenne and maple syrup and lemon juice, plus liquor, but can I drink it, *no*, and farther over the bar where the Japanese Commercial Print Photographer keeps drinking Roy Rogers and telling about the real-deal-Indian-Witchdoctor who showed him how he would die one day but gave him a silver-trinket belt buckle to keep him from it (this guy rubbing it in, showing off that he has what I've always wanted, knowing that he is safe and will never die, and if he does die, he will be protected by the Spirit of the Universe, given to him direct from a myth of the West of Indians of the American blood-in-us of the Indians, of the wild romp of the storytelling West, and he has it and I am anxious as shit with myself nuts as nuts, and this story is just some dumb story I wrote for the first story I wrote in the teacher's class, and I never got it approved of, but here it is, the worst one in the book—I'll try and find something in here to spruce up and make into a story for you, you incorrigible needy wild brain of a person, seeking the heart of the meat of life, which I can and cannot give)—and to the door, over the heads of the waiters and waitresses, past the bottles of wine and water and the bread baskets—beyond the tiled floor with the table legs rising—out to where there are no more mosaics or passageway arches, the windows open where the shutters extend and air passes from the bar into the street—there on the sidewalk is a man struggling to bring himself back into his wheelchair; he is setting his wheel locks and he grunts as he swings the chair upon its casters, arm-crawls on his chest on the sidewalk, him double-checking the clamps across the wheels, he groans, with his belly and groin and legs all dragging, pulling himself against the weight of failed parts, trying to lift himself, his chest, to seat level, reaching for one padded armrest he grips the cushion in the rain—but he slips, a hand upon the vinyl padding slips, and he falls with his chin cutting across one silver footplate, scraping his neck and face as he moans to the traffic and the headlights, but no one stops to help him, arms flexed, fists drawn together, neck corded, he shouts but only to submit back onto his back, humping, dragging himself across the grime, first there is all this—first there is this—but this is not first because before this, before this man and his chair and sidewalk, before the bar and me sitting at the bar, watching the kids running down the street until one collides into the back of the man's wheelchair and the man is jostled, struggling admirably, before all this, there is the waitress and I am out there looking for parking, en route to see her, because I should first say I am seeing her; I should tell you I am (was) seeing this waitress (so simple I was then, so young and stupid, now I have engines to learn, whole wheel assemblies, axles, transmissions, real things, new books to write, if I ever write another, so much lost, but still the great city in the darkness propelling me to get on the viatic trip and ride), apron, black pants, black shoes, whose name is Maesa, but she is not first, because first is not her, first there is me, the I of this story, and I am first, selfishly, unavoidably, using Maesa for a place to stay in old NYC (before meeting Catherine) and more sex and driving through the Village alone and finding nowhere to park, trying to get to where Maesa works and to park, but I hardly know the Village at all; my father knows the Village well, grew up here, and so maybe my father is first, but how can a father be first when a mother could really come first, and surely a father can't know a thing about being first such that a mother does (wrong!), and so certainly Mother must come first, and always did, with her fortune and her man's belt and powder case, and if Mother comes first then perhaps women come first in this story, and if women come first, then Maesa—but before Maesa, her own mother then, and so this is to get ahead of ourselves, as you will see, because Maesa's mother means exactly the round woman suffocating in a photograph on Maesa's wall, ahead of ourselves now we are, tubes up the nostrils and her in a wheelchair, too, back getting her photograph taken, and so now there is no way but to get ahead of things and say I was with Maesa this night long past when the man was thrown from his wheelchair, after I had been sitting at the bar and saw what happened to the man, and I thought to go and help him and did not and knew that my father, certainly my father would have helped this man because my father is a good man, a Christian man, although he was born something like a Jew, Fatherkovitch, but met Jesus or found faith, after he found drugs, and when he had found drugs was back running around the Village over the same streets as this restaurant is cornered, Maesa's restaurant, with the Japanese Print Photographer in his tight t-shirt still yack-yack-Yakatori-yacking at me, cartoon bird on his chest, and the man in the wheelchair struggling to rise, pitifully, strongly, on the same sidewalk where as a boy my father went running curly-haired, and one day stopped running and looked at his young foot and saw that it was made of glass and he saw a goldfish swimming inside his foot and this was when he was still very young, and America was aware in the heart, and he was excited to have a pet goldfish and he was eating dope all the time, in that time before me I am always trying to imagine, and I thought I would imagine better one day, but have not, and have found myself farther from—(as it must be for my father now) back then my dad was in the Rockies of Canada, those purple white topped hills under the blue of sky (where Brother Carl caught the trout), lost one night under the sky and stars, and someone gave him a Bible and said, "Take this and yada yada," and that was all, he had found Jesus Christ and himself and he is a good man, my father, and certainly he would have helped that man on the sidewalk, let's not forget this man is real, now, or was—and on the sidewalk, and I was not helping, not helping, watching, only, although I had thought to help him but was too afraid since so much was happening all at once and what if the man had something in his pants, a needle I thought, and I got prodded, pricked, or if he became violent with me or any number of things and anyhow weren't you supposed to be able and fend for yourself in this town, then I thought about my brother, Carl, who is also first before me (he was still alive when I wrote this worst story in the book, and I didn't save him, and I was insane to write, but you have to learn one part of the motor coach at a time, when you are nuts, when you have the itch, when you are bound to go down with America, in pursuit), and certainly my brother would have helped the man since my brother Carl is strong and lives in Oregon and anyone from Oregon would help anyone (see how dumb I was, what a kid? Having no idea we'd lose him)—especially a cripple in a wheelchair—who of course had no real power to harm me, I thought, and my brother rides a motorcycle the size of a mule and smokes cigarettes and packs a 9 millimeter and a smile to disarm the world with his big shoulders and genuine face and long Christ-like Buddha nature and his curls, and wouldn't go to the bathroom anywhere but his own place, not to take a dump, and would laugh and laugh at anything, and was so strangely himself, a great man with his St. Bernard, and his motorcycle, and his pistols, and his pot and his drinking and his great giant heart and laughing, and surely this man would not harm ME, and then I thought perhaps otherwise, and didn't know but what if it had been my mother sitting at the restaurant, what would she have done—who knows, other than she would have made a big production, made a speech and been seen, would have sermonized (trying to give the world something she has found, too, her delusion, her desire to show and to do and to make and to take hold, though maybe she would surprise me, as she has done all my life, and go help him, put her hands on his, be human which she has done), and if her parents had been there, certainly they would have done something to help, my grandparents from Ohio so clean and sharp, or made Shy the bartender do it, my grandmother would have said to him, My God, Shy, YOU do something, the man is hurt, you are strong, or my grandfather would have helped the man and then she would point this out, too, saying, 'Look he's however many years old, etc.,' but then maybe he would do nothing since he had a once terrifying incident down in New Orleans when he was a boy and besides he's eighty-three-or-so years (the same age as my teacher) and only about five-eight which definitely isn't big enough to help a broken man who needs to be lifted up into his wheelchair and who is shouting at the whole world of the Village and also my grandfather looks like a handsome millionaire turtle with white hair combed over and bottle glasses but he's no joke and everyone knows that's not the sort of man to…but I could have helped that man, seeing as how I am six-foot-seven-and-a-half and had not even moved from my seat with the Japanese man showing me his belt-buckle again, for the howmanyth time, so proud he wouldn't have to die, he wouldn't have to die, from a real Indian Witchdoctor (me still all flipped out on peyote, which now is just a little squeak and wink and the knowledge that there is nothing that cannot be surmounted, and there is no death, I pray, plus all the heat waves of vision), and out came Maesa flirting by and she was giving me the eye-lined-sex-eye while this woman in the corner was giving some man the sex eye and I was thinking how there was no way to try and make things work with Maesa, suddenly, when I just only wanted everyone to get away, back off, and give me some room, to be clean, again, and to be alone in the desert at night, tingling, but when I conferred this upon her later on—how I wanted to get alone from her, everyone, everybody, Maesa started crying and we struggled for hours in this really pathetic sort of fight that lasted too long and didn't get to any point and in the middle of fighting she wasn't wearing anything but these high-over-her-hipbone panties and I got interested and said I took it all back, "I take it all back," I said, and put my punctuation inside her so that we were having unsafe sex again, as lately I've been having this thing with the caps and inside Maesa on her giant comfortable bed I looked over and there was the picture of a sort of old woman, not too old, tubes running out her nose and rotund, obviously not going to last, I figured, and was it a really recent photograph, no, which I could tell from the hair and dress and the color, etc., and fading, and when we were done, not because we had cum in ecstatic leaps but because Maesa started crying again, I asked her who that woman was with the tubes out of her nose and it turned out, sure enough, her mother, collapsed lung, lung died and mother started smoking cigarettes and died altogether which made Maesa cry even more in my arms and I started rubbing her back absent-mindedly, as my father always did for my mother, before she left, my mother I am saying, and I started thinking about when I die and suddenly it was happening—there was this big Native Chief in the desert with a raised mound of dirt and he pointed to the SKY and said, "He wants to talk to you," and he had a look about him, like stones, like knowing things, like an old river, and blew a whistle of eagle bone, "you dumb shit," he said and pointed up again, and I went up and God was huge and fat and smoking a black cigar and laughing so I could either start laughing, too, or be left out of the joke entirely and so I started and he said, "You're done, Pal." And I said, "Great!" and hoped he'd like me and we went into this white space and I was about to disappear when I looked down and Maesa was still crying and there I was having a hell of a time as usual—thinking about dying and meeting with Indian Chiefs and smoking black cigars with God and suddenly it was then too late and I was back in my body on the bed feeling guilty (now, let me ask you, do you think I now think of dying? No. I am here for the duration. I am here to help and to be here for the ones I love, who will go before me, and I will be there, standing, throwing up inside, weeping in love with the earth and the spirit of life and all that horseshit, meaning I will be there holding the handle and walking through church, throwing up inside, meaning I will be here, for each person who needs me, anytime, to make up for my inability in every other respect of living) so I started scratching her back again and realized that this very woman with the fishtubes up her nose was who Maesa had come from, and it hit me then that Maesa's mom had come first before Maesa and I remembered Maesa telling me her father had been told to leave by Maesa's mother and then Maesa's mother died and Maesa was just about fourteen or so and suddenly she had no father and no mother and was on her own ever since and I thought, Jesus Christ, everything is fit to go wrong with this girl trying to make me into her mother and father at once and she'd take anyone and I remembered the man outside his wheelchair who I didn't help, so much to speak of, but did go stand next to and watched him struggle awhile and asked him if he needed anything, or some help, standing six-foot-seven or six-foot-seven-point-five inches beside him, and I remembered, holding Maesa in bed (after the sex, during which I was thinking all the wrong words, panicking with my insane Peyote nervous break down shit) how he had said to me, with the light from the streetlamps orange and making the world look so slow, the shadows smaller, a little eagle tattoo on his arm, "You think I need help from you? You think I need anything from *YOU*? Like I'm the one who's crippled and you're the *ONE* who rides the elephant? Well let me tell you, Boy, we are all cripples down here. Cripple heart. We all! Each and every one of us. To the damn death," he said and started laughing so I started laughing and he lit a black cigar and he smoked it, smoking and smoking and smoking until there was nothing but near white, and I could see nothing except smoke and I was so glad to be out there, with him, all alone past the tables and chairs and the couples fighting and Maesa crying, and my mother with the children running down the street and the bottles of wine and the Japanese fellow yapping and all the bread in the baskets, as many as they could fill, overflowing with bread, and Shy the bartender and my grandparents smiling and waving, and Carl riding his machine, and my kid sister, Marie, always a genius and really I just truly missed my father a tiny bit, there in the smoke, feeling myself disappearing—my real father—and I wished I could see my grandfather one last time; wished I could see everyone again like I had wanted in that peyote ceremony, as I have ever since I was a boy, as a man even, to see my father and grandfather and America and suddenly I thought back to it all and whispered, 'So long, I'm heading off, Cocksuckers. Thanks for everything, Cocksuckers. Thank you. Thanks so terribly much. Thanks for nothing! It's been real. I'm off! Gone.

THE MINDS OF BOYS

IT WAS STILL summer and the days had been long forever. The moon was a long stretch of yellow and the waves sparkled on the blackened sea. Keiko was wrestling a dog. The new dog that Other had lured to camp that afternoon.

"It's simple," Keiko told Other, back at the store's back parking lot. "You're going in the store and you're going to steal some meat. Good raw meat. Black Styrofoam trays of meat. Once you get it, we'll cover you with meat juice, pin strips of meat onto you, and you'll go running through the park. Whatever dogs chase back are ours."

It was of no use to argue. Keiko was the boss. And he was old, though he claimed to be sixteen. He was a big guy, with huge hairy thighs squeezed into a pair of old black bathing shorts.

"This is going to be great," Keiko said. "This means more dogs for us. Hot poopoo. Piss!"

In the moonlight, Keiko and the new dog struggled for control. The dog howled and Keiko made sharp cracking sounds, landing elbows or fists to the dog's side and head. The troop watched from a distance, their fire burning itself in the wind. They didn't circle in to watch Keiko as they had earlier in the summer, when Keiko punched and the new dogs fought with their teeth, with vigor and honor and braveness.

The boys knew this from experience, and they didn't want to watch. Instead they drank warm beer in cans, sipping slowly, and licked their upper lips for moisture. Not one had enough lip fuzz to catch any drop-sized glints of beer, but they licked anyway, imagining mustaches and the tickle of wet hairs on their tongues.

Winds came and swept the ash off the coals, making their fire burn brighter. Flames cast long shadows across the sand, and waves roved across the grainy sea. Keiko punched and the new dog growled. Then cried. Some of the boys wished silently for the dog.

"Dog sounds alright," Other said.

"Yeah," some boys agreed. Earlier that day, they reclined and watched the sky as big as anything, happy to have time in the world.

A billowy cloud had been shaped like a whale and another was a long feather but also a dragon-shaped sword, and then there were streaks of white that blended. At night, the clouds were ash and smoke. The dark was close beside them, kept back only by the rise and fall of firelight in wind. The booming of waves in the surf.

In the morning they would find a band of blackened sand and cool chunks of charcoal. In the mornings, they never missed their mothers. But at night, sitting and listening to a dog get hurt, some longed for home.

"Let's go to that dance," Cutlass said. "The one those girls were talking about." Worm agreed. So did Gill. Cutlass seemed most ready to go, his wingborn curls mooning out from his face. He cut his hair with a knife whenever he wanted, and now he was ready to go. But they couldn't go unless Keiko agreed.

Other laughed, "Are you kidding? Keiko will never let us." But no one seemed to pay attention. They heard the dog cry and saw it run sideways from Keiko. He started back toward the fire. Closer, the flames lit Keiko and they could see he was bleeding.

"What are you looking at?" Keiko said, slick with dog slobber and grease. He spit into a palm and rubbed his bleeding hand through his hair.

"Any you going to wrestle the new dog?" he said. "No? What are you so quiet for? All miss your mothers?"

"We want to go to this dance tonight," Cutlass said, but Keiko just laughed. He inspected his hand, sucked at the wound. "None of you gonna wrestle? Not one?"

"There's going to be girls at it."

"Girls! What do you need them for?"

"I don't. But haven't you ever wanted to know about them? What they smell like?"

"What they smell like? Lick your own hand and smell it. That's all."

Cutlass looked into the fire and he felt sorry. He wanted to lick his hand to smell it, but he would have to wait until no one was looking.

They started all talking about the dance, roaming in line from tallest to short to medium and then to shortest of all. They were dark and silhouetted by the moon, tromping away from the fire and farther from the sea.

Keiko led because Keiko always led, and Other followed.

Behind Other was Cutlass. And behind Cutlass was Gill. Behind Gill was Worm. And behind Worm was Void. Then came Baxal. After Baxal followed Chance, smoking a cigarette that was mostly just filter. He dug them up on the beach or picked them off the ground at the store's back parking lot.Bean was last, the youngest of all. And after Bean came one of the rotten dogs. Bean chased the dog off with a stick.

"Look at that cloud," Cutlass said, mouth holding a wad of spit. Then he spit the spit as far as he could, arching so the moon was in his sights. For a moment the whole beach smelled like how he imagined a girl would. Then the dog came back and Bean chased it with the stick.

They reached the parking lot and saw the gymnasium with its orange external lights protected by metal cages. They made toward the stairs and Keiko circled back to the end of the line to be last. He tried to slip through the doors, but the chaperones moved and blocked the entrance.

"Where do you think you're going?"

"In."

"Surely not," said the woman chaperone. "This is a preteen dance."

"Good thing I'm preteen, then." Keiko went to push her. A man stood between them with his arms. "Alright, Mac," he said. "What are you trying to pull?"

"Look, I'm fifteen. I have a hormone imbalance. Those are my friends."

"You're bleeding," said the man. "You got school ID?"

"Home-schooled."

"Sorry. But you're not getting in," the man said. "This is a secure area."

"I'll remember you," Keiko said and he glared, rubbing the bite mark on his face. "I'll remember," he said, but sounded more sad than threatening. There was bullying and sexting and terrorism and things for chaperones to worry about—shootings—God, good chaperones had plenty to worry about.

Inside the boys were looking around, letting their eyes adjust to the lights. They had spent their summer around campfires, and for the first time they were back inside a school gymnasium.

They saw girls—wearing tube tops with scalloped straps, padded bras pushing their little cleavages up toward soft necklines. The boys could smell the scented lotions, the deodorant sprays, and the chewing gum they thought was from the girls' sweat. These girls lived in houses. Boys woke in the dunes, where they hid, far down the coast in the grass—with a new dog sleeping by their face, fur rank with mildew and salt. Sometimes it was Keiko they woke beside, his big thighs up against them, but here were real girls, eighth graders. Some wearing black skirts and pantyhose, bright lipsticks and gold jewelry. Plus interesting footwear. Blue towel-looking shoes with big cork bottoms, and shiny red platforms with open-toe fronts, three toes squeezed together. There were plastic ones with hard bows that made the girls' calves push up. Some wore strappy numbers and stood on pencil-thin sticks. War was fine anywhere else if America had footwear like this! Some girls had white toe-nail polish on the ends of their toenails, and some reminded Cutlass and Gill of sisters back home.

With Keiko, every morning had its chores: finding wood, stealing food. It was good living at the beach. There were structures to build up and old ones to tear down, dogs to steal and return for rewards. There were all sorts of grand adventures—swim races in the sea—and a time each day to sit and ponder questions like how far the sky was from the ground or if dreams weighed anything in their brains at night. America had been getting funny. Families all were heartbroken in weird houses. But the whole world was at the beach, free.

Here were girls, thin-limbed and covered in little hairs. Their eyebrows tweezed to nothing. Others had eyebrows thick as birds' wings. Here were women.

Keiko stood in the parking lot and scratched at a thigh. He looked up and saw a cloud like a head with a moon going through it like a torch.

"Think Keiko's alright?" Other said, but nobody responded. They were each taking in the view.

Glum girls stood against the wall and looked away, striking their butts against the painted cinderblocks. The good-lookers all stood in a circle on center court and inside the circle was a girl wearing a brace. It started down at her collarbones and held bars that rose up and attached to pins sticking out of her skull. She looked caged inside there. And her eyes moved. She'd been shot accidently in the neck by a stray bullet from a helicopter on her way to school one day. She would wear the brace until spring.

The troop neared and she said, "Watch out! Don't let them bump." The other girls stared at the boys' torn clothes and their filthy hands, but noticed also how darkly tanned and the way the boys were looking at them and weren't afraid. Girls liked Cutlass's haircut. Void rubbed his knees and Gill put his hand in a pocket. He started to move it inside and walked over to the saddest-looking girl against a wall.

Chance, Worm, Baxal, Bean, and Cutlass were all trying to figure which girls would be easiest to dance with, and which were tall enough, so that while dancing they could put their hands low on the girls' waistlines and let their fingertips graze the highest point of their smooth bottoms.

Cutlass was first to approach the circle of girls. Worm, Baxal, Chance, Void, and Bean were watching.

"You girls still live with your mothers," Cutlass announced, not like a question.

"Where else?" the girl with the neck scoffed, and another girl in a bright yellow tube top said, "Yeah." This was one Cutlass didn't think would be easiest to dance with. Plus she was short.

"We have quit our mothers," Cutlass said. "We live down at the beach with our friend Keiko. We're thieves. We stay up drinking beer, have fires, and we steal whatever we want. We've come to take you with us."

"That's lame," the girl with the broken neck said. But another girl with hair on her lip said, "Cool."

"Yeah," Cutlass said, "very cool. You want to dance with us?"

"With all of you?" she laughed like he'd made some sort of mistake. Cutlass did not laugh. He had not made a mistake. "With me first, then we'll see," he took her hand and it was soft. He moved her away from the rest of them. Together they swayed. Cutlass hooked the tips of his thumbs together, and put his hands low on the girl's waistline.

"What's your name?

"Clementine."

"Really?"

"Yes, really."

"Why?" Cutlass asked.

"I don't know, what's yours?"

"Mine's Cutlass."

"Like the car?"

"Sure, like the car. What else?"

She smelled of nail polish and chocolate. Her hair was up in a waterfall and his fingers felt dirty.

The other boys from the troop were soon dancing, and each couple was dancing differently.

Bean was so short that his nose reached up only above the waist of the girl he was dancing with, and Cutlass, seeing this, wondered how Bean had ended up with the tallest of the girls. Worm had his partner in a sort of headlock and was skipping wildly in place. Gill was grinding with the sad-looking girl in the corner. Somehow, a ring of couples had formed around the girl with the neck who was standing in the center of them all, protected from any further harm that could be occasioned upon her.

"We've got us a real nice beach," Cutlass told Clementine. "Our friend Keiko's probably getting us more beer. You smell like nail polish, you know?"

"Thanks."

"You girls can come with us."

"Can we just dance a bit?"

"Fine. But I like you. You're coming."

Terrorism was big lately. There were increases in security. The girls felt good and the boys didn't care about NAFTA.

Mexico and bullfights would be a thing in their futures. Fuck terrorism.

Keiko was back from the store with a full case of cans. He saw a young girl with black braids and dark nail polish smoking a whole cigarette and offered her a beer.

"You know, I'm not as old as I look," Keiko said.

"Well, you seem old."

"I can fight dogs. No problem."

"Dogs?"

"Back at the beach. We've got a camp and I wrestle. You should come."

"This is good beer." She had never had a whole beer.

"Look. I'm their leader. This whole troop of guys inside idolizes me. We live at the beach and I take care of them. I try not to hurt the dogs. I'm trying to talk to you." She squinted and really looked at his face for the first time. He looked focused.

"Meet my new dogs, come to the beach. Haven't you ever been with a man with beer on the beach? No! Well, let's go." He was so excited. He would never die—all heart and goodness.

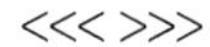

(Like my brother, Carl. These words, these stupid words. My heart my brother, my first friend, my amigo, my miss, I miss, oh, the dumb earth. You should have seen him. You'll never know. Or you do. He and his friends at a campfire in a backyard in Oregon. The big pine trees in his yard on the East Side, somewhere near Mt. Tabor. Near the house where he was found. Us all as in life, in the firelight, all alive. All accounted for. Him drinking bottles. Me smoking smoking smoking. No plan but the life ahead, long as could be imagined.)

<<< >>>

The chaperones warned how they would not be allowed back in, but everyone was talking and hollering and the girls were saying, 'For a little bit only.' 'Just one beer.' And 'Where do you get the beer?' And 'What about your parents?' 'Aren't they worried?' And the boys said, 'We don't care,' though some really did. Hardly, though, with the girls!

When they neared the beach, Clementine was riding on Cutlass's back and her little breasts jiggled in her padded bra. Bean rode on the tallest girl's back and was mock-kicking her in the kidneys as if wearing spurs. Gill hadn't even left the dance and was still grinding against the saddest girl in the corner.

They got closer and Baxal said, "Shhhhhh." They saw an outline of Keiko on top of some little creature by the fire. The boys first thought it was a dog. Then they knew it was a person.

Keiko wasn't being mean. He had a girl under him and her head was on the sand. She was whispering to Keiko and touching his face. Her fingers were thin and her black nail polish lit shiny by the flames, and she smoked with a long thin hand.

"What do you see in the clouds?" Keiko asked her.

"I see a whale over there. That one's like a turtle. That feather-looking cloud looks like a sword, and that one looks like a dog. What do you think they look like?"

"The boys are all gonna leave me and then the dogs will run away."

"Keiko, you know I can't be your girlfriend," the girl said and made a face and Keiko jerked his face towards her.

"Then what are you even doing here?"

"Keiko," Cutlass said, "we've come to watch you wrestle the dogs!"

"I know," Keiko said, "I know. I know you have. And you brought the girls to watch. Now I won't do it."

"What do you mean? You always wrestle. These girls have come to see."

"Then tonight I don't," he said and got up from the girl and walked towards the sea. They didn't know what he was doing. He was big looking, even out in the silver hoop of wet, splashing in the final roll of waves.

They watched him push out into the deep, beyond the reach of firelight. Barely there in the moonlight, he was using his heft against the dark water.

The dogs got up from the circle and followed him out.

In the waves, dogs caught him and grabbed his arms with their teeth. He kept pushing out but the dogs stayed afloat, covering his head and arms, maybe trying to rescue him. The boys heard him groan, and watched him fight, but soon there was nothing but dark waters and a pack of wild dogs floating on the sea.

"Keiko!" Cutlass screamed out. "Come back, now."

The rest shouted his name, and waited for him to rise from the surface.

Eventually, dogs came back from the sea and lay upon the sand by the fire to dry. No one said a word. The clouds sank before the moon, and the beach grew even darker, except for a small circle of firelight. Then a great wind rose up and stole the ash from off the coals, and they glowed hot in their red and cracking shapes. Each one in the party stared into the fire. And they all saw different things, creatures and animals and skulls, swords and ships, teeth and heads and all the forms that have existed now and always, but mostly in the minds of boys.

GIRLS IN HEAT

YOU'VE HEARD it all, but here comes one more. I'll be the first to admit you've heard all I have to tell you. You are not new to this world. Look, I'll be the first and the second and so forth to give away all hope of telling you what is new about the world you have seen all of, etc.,—birds and sky and those big clouds in the southwest and everywhere really that stack up infinitesimally high like a god even after you have seen it all already. It's a miracle. I'll try not and trick you, and this circling is not going on in circles, but my dog's you-know-what is the size of a clementine right now, and she's six months. Pussy. The man I got her from, and his fiancée, they said she was spayed. They had a text sign off message that says Mr. and Mrs. Stewart. So every time I used to get a text from them I was confused as to who they thought I was, and why they would call me Mr. and Mrs. Stewart, and then that, too, I caught onto and nothing is new about that now. I told you about that couple. Well, didn't I? Well, she isn't spayed. That isn't anything new my having been fooled. But her (dog?) vagina is the size of a tangerine. I mean, a small orange. It has popped out and she's such a little thing, a delicate creature, who reminds me so much of my love who has left me—Catherine. This is not new either. You've heard of Catherine by now from me if you have heard anything from me by now. I know there's not anything new about being so in love with a woman and her leaving a man for a Manuel.

I am so much a fool as to have thought, as she met him in Paris, that he was French. Manuelo French. Can you believe that? I thought forever he was French, but then one day she tells me he is Spanish. Manuel Spanish! She had kept that from me, but that isn't new, my being in the black. Now I hate Spanish and French alike. I'd like to give every small boy in Western Europe a black eye. A real popper. You have your life. Come on. You maybe might have had a dog by now. Maybe you've been in love. Hoodwinked. Snookered.

Jewely is my dog.

I'm in a Ramada hotel, where I paid nearly 100 dollars to stay because I didn't want to try and drive home to the ranch where I live an hour drive from Dallas and there's not much to make me want to do much. I just rented the room. So, my puppy, she has her pussy all swollen out like the miniature cuff of a man's dress shirt, and her tail moves from side to side and I look at her and I look away and here's where I'm sure I'll lose some face, and here's where I say the wrong thing, but I keep looking at her like this, in heat, and I can nearly feel how it feels for her and I keep thinking of Catherine. I can't stop thinking about Catherine. They both move somewhat in a graceful way, Jewely being part husky (dingo, really) and in the tradition of the wolf, and Catherine being a wolf of sorts, so sleek, her hair a Colorado storm, and something about how neither of them want to ever be seen going to the bathroom, and how they move so delicately and with such power and grace, and I can find some nishy now and then but I can't lay with a girl or woman afterward. I can't stand to anymore. My heart is elsewhere. (Can you believe this doddering smut? I could have called him! I could have picked up for Oregon and saw him instead of writing these dumb words. Instead of this!) It's something about it. I don't like the fucking after having had real love and the lying afterwards together is nothing awfully romantic. Hairy legs and eyes looking all over. I see Jewely and I told Catherine earlier today on the phone that Jewely is in heat. Catherine is about to menstruate, she told me over the telephone. Jewely is in heat. These are the women in my life. My girls in heat. I won't go into the others that I have tried to date recently. You've been around. I'm in a hotel with striped wallpaper, and a storm is darkening the sky. I was out a moment ago and smoked ciggies and the rain fell on my shoulders. It was the big rain that soaks your shirt with a few drops, and I was out there in the first rain of the Texas summer, smoking under an overhang, and with the door propped to the hallway and then standing in the hallway smoking and blowing the smoke out the door. I saw the reflection of the drops on my shirt.

Inside my room is Jewely. She keeps licking herself and she moves differently now. It is worth the hundred dollars, nearly, to have had that moment in the summer rain.

I am so I don't like to talk to anyone so much anymore. I like the rain like that. I have seen the world. A smell. A feeling of wetness on the shoulders. Catherine is still with Manuel. I can tell you that I will never stop loving her. You've been here in the world, have you not? You've been in a hotel? There's nothing else.

AMERICA, AMERICA, AMERICA

LISTEN, people find a way to get even with a guy. I have the story on this note. I was over at the hardware store talking to Carl Daeson. Carl is a big fat old boy in Texas and he was helping me to find a part to go around the hookups for the washer and dryer in the ranch I rent.

Some people are just big around fat porkers, big guys, I mean, they make you sad to see them—I am saying their faces do. There is so much to them, so much whole life in them, and heart, and it makes you want to put your face into them and it breaks your heart to look at them.

I had to cover up and patch this rat hole a wood rat had made inside the wall at Squeaky's ranch. I rent the ranch from this big gay roper, Squeaky. (Here! I told you I'd get back to Squeaky.) He and I had it all out the other day and now I have to move out and first I have to fix this rat hole that enormous rat made while I was back up where I belong up North, moving—I was moving my dead...what is even the right word for this unspeakable thing I can't get my mind around—I was moving my brother's things out of his house. Up in Oregon. Carl. His name was Carl, is Carl, Carl. He was a big guy, the best guy, all calm peaceful but tough and drinking a certain kind of whiskey, two kinds I know them both, and motorcycles and a laugh like Christmas was today and you were the best thing he'd ever set eyes on. Like you were his brother. Hey, if you can't stomach it, my stories, when the book is over I'll tell you the one I didn't put in the book. Call me. My number is on the flap. On the internet. All over. Here's my name: _______________. Want me to spell it?

There I was standing with Carl Daeson—my brother's first name—standing there figuring how to fit this plastic frame over the square where the hookups come through the wall to cover up the softball sized hole in the wall which a rat chewed as well as chewed through the plastic framing for the square in the wood paneling where the hookups come through for the washer and dryer.

Squeaky comes over the other Friday and we have a showdown at the ranch and he's drunk and the place is a stinking mess. Full of rat holes I guess he couldn't see because he was drunk and his eyes were a mess and he stood there fuming around with his barrel chest and blazing red neck and squeaky voice looking at how my toilets aren't scrubbed free of urine and my clothes are all over the floor and my dirty videos on the dresser and cigarettes stamped out in the wooden bowls his dead mother left he and his dad—Squeak's brother is dead, too. The whole ranch used to have furniture out front on the front porch that's rotting off and ashtrays everywhere and photos of Squeak and his big brother, handsome in cowboy hats and lariats on their sides on their white and golden horses. Two brothers grinning as in a photograph on one wall of the ranch. Like that old Camel man with the curly hair lighting up another old cig. Like America, I mean. The last bit of the unbreakable America that lives. That was me and my brother, too, just like this. But then you understand it's me now at the ranch only.

When I came back from Oregon, that old king rat was dead on my counter, that big wood rat, neck snapped and dried blood was pooled around and stuck to the trap and the fur on the thing, and the first item I noticed was the smell of death and I was wearing my brother's clothes and standing around sobbing all alone in the living room looking at the kitchen and out the window like someone was going to come down the long road and give me a hug, which didn't happen. Do I have to tell you? I'd never been to a funeral before I carried my brother in a church. WE are Catholic. American. Wild. Lunatics. We've been far out. Now I'm here in the ranch. SHIT!

I sat down on the couch and tried to smoke but couldn't.

So I understand the stains in the toilets and why the wooden bowls Squeaky's mother loved and used for salad in the summer upset him and why he wasn't happy with me, him drawling away and lurching about like he was, but don't kid yourself, I've never been handsome on a horse with a lasso. [Want to hear what I read on a menu in Portugal that broke my heart the same week my brother died, and I had no way to know he would: *Omelet with french fries and salad.* In English. On a menu.] Besides, there I stood a younger brother just like him, with no clue on going on and I'm no kid anymore, don't kid yourself, but have I figured out what to do? Or has Squeaky? Give me a joke! No.

Squeaky is a four time International Gay Rodeo Association Grand Champ and will probably sue me for writing about him and using his name. His name is on the internet. I think he switched electrical boxes on me from one house to the other. I met him by calling a real estate sign for a different house and telling the guy what I wanted. He said no and hung up. Then called back an hour later. Offered me Squeaky's place. Told me how to get there, didn't know my name, told me to go inside if I wasn't afraid of dogs. I went in and called the guy and said I'd take it. He said Andy and Squeaky would move out and live in his back house. I didn't understand a thing about what was going on. I didn't even know what "roper" meant when the real estate agent told me about Squeakers and Andy being ropers. Squeaky still has my brother's A/C unit that was very expensive and stands in the middle of a room and I still owe Squeaky 300 dollars. Let that be entered as evidence in the courtroom wherein Squeaks sues me. Whatever you get, Squeak! Plus 300 buckaroos, Buckaroo. Upon giving me back my damn A/C.

I left the Ace Hardware and went to the Soap Sponge to wash the truck. I'm getting long winded.

I finished washing and no miracles had happened all day but sun and the wispy clouds of an October day in Texas lilting around up there sort of gay up in the sky. Plus I worked all morning at my job, trying to convince college students I advise that there's something to this world anymore even though I wouldn't plan on it. I go over to the vacuum machines that charge you a dollar and fifty cents just to move air through a tube. I start sucking away the Jewely dog hair inside the truck and sucking up the dirt in the cup holders and sucking the cracks in the leather seats where the sand from the ranch collects. You want some advice? I don't have any. And into the stall next to me pulls a car with these two women inside and one is younger and she hops out of the car-door closest to me and has tight jeans on with no front pockets but the lines like front pockets stitched on but no pockets at all, which is the new thing, I guess, because they aren't even jeans, and the back of the jeans covered in sequins making crosses on either ass cheek, both cheeks, sparkling like that in the Texas sun.

She's got a shirt on that's an eagle in sequins. A little skin above the waistline and hipbones and some thighs. I'm thinking I haven't had any touching in so long I've started to count the months. She starts sucking away, having paid her money, and she's sucking up the crumbs and hair and little french fries and sequins and what have you. So...here is the part I've been getting to. I start thinking it over and then I say,

"Hey, why don't you let me? I mean, why don't you get a good man like me to do that work for you?"

She looks at me and she thinks for a second, and the sucking is running, so that's money ticking away. Then says, "Okay, have at it," and sticks the hose at me and I take it and start sucking the cracks and getting into the grooves. It's just her and this other woman in the front, who is big, too, but who is not the fat to make the heart swim, as she has got the fat inside her to turn mean and you could see that from her face. Oh, God, sometimes the world drags you over the coals and all you can do is get a good handful of skin and pull it away from your heart, and try to get that heart as close to the coals as possible. Or cover it in fat. I want to live in the past or die. How is that getting close to the coals? The world has done it for me, or I have, or haven't, who knows? What has it done? Who?

Well, guess who comes up driving in his truck? Squeaky! He climbs out of his truck cab and starts shouting me up and down because he'd snuck into the ranch while I was over at the hardware store and found that rat hole bigger than a baseball. Actually, he says it's as big as a baseball. The girl gets in the car and the other drives them away. Then Squeaky tells me he's going to keep my deposit on the ranch he already charged me, and he leaves. I am hot. I'm sweating through my shirt. I'm thirsty and alone. In nowhere East Texas. It hits me like a ton of dirt. I have no idea what I'm doing out here in America, America, America. What should I do? I'd decided I'd just go and fix that rat hole back at the ranch, I thought, the one I had to move out of anyhow. I love Squeaky if you didn't notice. So, there it was. Isn't it just like I say it is? Don't people find a way to get back at you? Well, don't they?

CHORES

YOU WILL PLAY THE PART of work. I work and you work. It is all about doing a little work on a Saturday. It's about a little housework, anyhow. It's about riding the up and down feelings. Remember when there was a house and you lived there with your father and mother and orange juice came in a cardboard tube with a lid? Remember seeing Mommy and Daddy, and you saw Daddy's penis and you were a boy and your mommy didn't have a penis, and you, little you, were Mommy and Daddy, and you and your daddy had penises and Mommy didn't. Or you were a little girl and you were also Mommy and Daddy, and you and Mommy had vaginas and Daddy had a penis from his? Well, there were chores to do then.

A little domestic chore time is what we are up to. You've done chores right? We all did chores, no? There were chores to do once. Remember the work that we had to do? Remember being a kid and having chores. I still have them, but I don't of course. I do what I want to do now, but I miss having those chores. I can go to restaurants at any time in the a.m. and eat and do whatever I like. Chores are what this has to do with you! You are me in the chores we might do on a Saturday afternoon. After rehabs. After jail. After love. After the big never ending loss.

The adventures are over! The adventures that led us to here and there and no more sailing around Puerto Rico on a motorbike, or running New York in search of the greatest editor of all times, the editor Gordon Lightning-running. The editor Cuff Cuff. The editor Solomon Everbloom. That great editor in the sky, up in the penthouse, up on the Upper East Side of Manhattan, up there smoking joints in his shorts, at his ivory table, me down below running amuck trying to get a postcard from him to say I am the one he's been waiting for, boy, to call me his boy, to call me up and say, 'You're my boy, Kid, you have spake like no one has ever spaken, German talk, so and so, you're the future of American Letters, etc.' How about a joke? Yes, I was running a muck waiting for my name to come out of his lips on paper, his Injun lips out of a wild leather jewboy grown insane face in New York reading Salinger, ripping off Salinger, wearing a hat with a feather I found for him, a Bald Eagle, me not naming it and not even having a face except for my face, wanting my name in lights, running wild all over with my face under lights, trying to really *wear* jeans, like a Colorado kid, a real live Kid, like so many men in jeans from Colorado from the famous stories of famous books that Solomon Everbloom read, and I read, and you read, and me trying to get myself some more pussy from Catherine while I didn't even have a face, falling so in love without a face, being seen by her and really being loved by her and suddenly being *Real* just as if my name really was in lights, trying to get an adventure, having an eagle land on my head, trying to find the Indians I knew from pictures under glass in grade school Ohio, where my brother Carl and I went to grade school, and my kid sister Marie, and but the adventure is over, Boy, it's time for chores. Here's the JOKE: A man tells his kid never to go into the adult bookstore. He says, "Don't go in there or you might see something you don't want to see." So here's the punchline. The kid goes in and there he finds his father! How do you like that? Having lived all over America. Having prayed. Having been nuts. Having been in rehabs, jails, having jumped and leaped from my brain with my body into the streets, now in a coat and tie, teaching college, with time off to go bananas.

Anyhow, the truck is a grey Ford in the sun. My shirt is off. It was when I thought of this.

You want to know what my big brother was like? He brought people to live in his home, he gave my father flowers on holidays, he walked around with sausages wrapped in paper towels in his pockets and shared them—he could smile so you understood Christ is better than books.

What it was that really got me to think of this, after all the time in New York City, the bars in New York City, the art shows in New York City, the cups of coffee in New York City, the blue and white paper cups of coffee that taste like coffee, the Library in New York City, the Catherine who looks better nude than any woman you've ever seen, the streets in New York City—the palm trees in San Francisco when I walked around with a bandaged foot and a golf club in San Francisco—where the ocean-bound bums covered Fulton or

Geary, where the Mission creeps along or rides on bicycles or bums dope or stomps in the streets, or on the streets of the Tenderloin where I walked faceless all night chasing prostitute transvestites for nothing but a look, too afraid to do anything but look, where I saw people living in broken down cars, where drunks wove through the night, down to Fillmore where the black dudes blared their music and the lights were all on in the buildings and I walked with my hands in my jeans with no face, for six years, and ended up in a Peyote hut with Indians I was too terrified to look at, as they knew what to do and I didn't, when I woke up without sleeping in the dawn of ice on ponderosa and horehound and the only love I found was Catherine and my own and my family—from the cardboard orange juice days of chores—and my brother's, Carl's, who I grew up with who had sad brown clean eyes and caught a fish through the eyeball on a first cast in the mountains of Montana. He caught it. Who with my sister we formed the three of us who could take it all and push onward. While fishing off a silent canoe. My father was there as a young father of ours and what got me thinking about this all was being shirtless and seeing the holes on the truck, the little black specks I mean on the truck.

My dog Jewely is out here.

Or was when I got the idea. The big willow is weeping in the wind, or was. It's a sunny day with the water hose in the grass and a blue bucket with a wash cloth and suds. I live in a neighborhood now. The first thing is to get the truck wet. Then you sink your hand into the soapy water in the cold bucket for the dish rag. Spray down the grey truck in the sun with the water from the hose. There is music to work by. A guitar then a voice. Drums. The drums keep the ground while the guitar travels out into the world beyond words. Then the singing gives us the heart, the gold Chalice that old Joyce wrote about and Gordon Lightrunning knows by heart in his golden heart all alone in his apartment on the Upper East Side eating steak. He wrote me a postcard once and it said I was a citizen for sure for finding him that Eagle Feather and for what I wrote about it, even though later he told me it was nothing to write home about. I showed everybody that story about the Feather. I showed it all over the place. It got me a bowl of soup, some nookie after Catherine left me for the Spaniard, and first place in a journal contest. Oh, and it got me a gig editing in NYC. Well, the singing is more than the guitar and the drums together. I have sprayed the truck with the back window cracked and water has gotten inside of my brother's truck which I have to take care of now. Sometimes, after the palm trees on Fulton and the Palm Trees at rehab number four, and the palm trees where my brother and I went as boys to see the old alligator they had to spray with a hose to get to move, and the palm trees on post cards, and all the while and all the adventure, and the stark raving around in jeans trying to be a real man with a face, and all the chores and the books and old Gordon Lightbloom, I can't hold it all in anymore and I have to look to the sky at the clouds and the blue and the drifty clouds of a Saturday at work and listen to the music and cry some of those tears that feel half-fake for as hard as I've tried to ride the horse with my guts, and to travel this globe, and to win old Catherine who I will never stop loving, and to be a good brother to my brother, and then I remember my big brother as big as any man around when I would hug him, and his curly long hair and motorcycle sunglasses and pistol in his pocket or truck, and him saying to me on the day I was leaving for my last adventure so far, him saying, "Why don't you just stick around, Man? Don't you want to just stick around and spend some time with me?" And how could I have known but I should have known what he was really saying. He was saying help me out, brother. Be here. But there I went like an idiot trying to mean something in the world with my name in lights and nothing but horseshit and there was the last time I saw my big brother until he was gone and I was carrying him through a church crying my eyes out and throwing up inside. So eat that, Lightbottom you editor from Hell. Life! It's not chasing old Catherine around. It's not kid stuff.

The music is the drum that holds you to the earth and your sex, desire, will and want to fuck and stay, the guitar takes you traveling, and the singing is the golden cup of feelings. Bells also do this. An album used to be an album, where we knew the musicians were making the impossible sounds of music—so we listened closely. I was listening closely to the music, and I had gotten the hood of the truck that is my brother's Ford all wet. I turned the spigot off on the side of the house. I turn the spigot and the water stops spraying on the brick house from the ring of the hose that attaches to the spigot. I had been to the hardware store in this small town in Texas and walked the aisles. Oh, boy, do they have stuff for chores. And so this is where it all ends. The eagles, the peyote, boy, did I tell you about the peyote? The way the ash spun in the air above the fire in the slowest spiral, and how I saw through my brain instead of my eyes, and still do. But the eyes didn't get it right. Moving everything. Do you know what it's like to try and really wear a pair of jeans after that? To really live in America? To be in East Texas, well, that's the only place to be after all! For a time. New York, give me a break? Do you know what New York looks like after the ash spun like that? You need a palm tree after that. I have no palm trees in the yard here in Texas. I have a yard to push a mower through, a manual mower! I still haven't figured out how to look at the sky since that episode with the Indians. But it doesn't matter now after my brother has died and I have to wash his truck and do some chores. Don't kid yourself. I'm licking wounds—but still kicking.

I remember picking up sticks.

That was one chore as a kid. Another was clean the garage. That was the worst one. You had to take all the bikes out of the garage. There wasn't much outside of that woods we lived in back then, except the moon, which was ours. I wanted too much. We had a gravel road that went from the woods to town. Night came and town was dark, boy, and no one was out. No one locked the doors. Everyone had a vacuum cleaner and a carpeted basement. Yes, a lot of beer to drink. Some packs of cigarettes. Some Marlboros, boy. Yes, there were no palm trees, but they were up in the moon. The moon was ours and Ohio was ours and we were boys in a woods and Dad would be happy to take a walk after some beers and stare up at that moon. The crazy man he was.

Or even go for a drive real slow or real fast down that gravel road to the lake. Have a few beers and sit at the end of a pier and watch the water and the moon rock, while I just sat there thinking crazy talk. But the point, the real point was taking everything out of the garage and sweeping it out. Taking the bicycles out, and the buckets, and the garbage cans, and the recycle bins, and the rakes and the shovels and the hockey stick and the basketballs and everything and then once it was swept out you had to wash the garage floor. The other chores were mowing. Also, weeding the brickwork and weeding the crab apple trees.

Yes, there were chores there to do on a Saturday. We were a family there in Ohio. And you? What chores? Who did you do them for? Now the sky, oh I still don't have that down!

Not looking at it. I haven't got that to a science. It's all up in the air to tell you the truth. It really is. But what could be more important than that sky now, boy? You should have had your hands on some of the beautiful girls I had my hands with and theirs on mine, but that's another story. The point is I got that postcard, and now I have a typewriter and chores because I am going to tell you about the truck and those little black dots of tar on the bottom sideboards of the truck which are really plastic, and on the wheel wells, which are plastic, too, and on the bumper especially, but there aren't tar balls there so much as little holes where the metal is rusting under the holes in the plastic of the bumper. I have turned off the spigot. I have plunged my hand into the bucket of soapy water. Your hand. I wish I could see your hand. See them both and hold onto them for a moment. I don't care if you are a man or a woman. I don't care how beautiful you are or how fat or hairy or strong, I don't really care. I've had fake ones and little ones and big real ones and mother's ones and all of them all over the world and licked a chest too and I tell you what, it's just as good to be doing chores now and taking care of this truck that I have to take care of and I'll tell you why, but you have to know that those holes in the bumper and those tar spots are like stars and I'm under the sky. It's a nice enough sky. I see spinning things up there. I see a man in the clouds standing over a typewriter. I see myself up there standing over the keys of this typewriter. I hear the music taking me places and keeping me on the ground and singing the golden heart of man singing to the point where he's feeling what he started singing and he won't stop feeling it and it's coming through.

But how on the ground can you be with your head six-feet-nine inches off the ground. Don't kid yourself, I'm not on the ground. I'm not even having a face except when I look in the mirror, and that's who? Go look at yourself. Who do you see? What'd you lose? What is the brightest you remember being? What are we forgetting?

I think he's singing about lost love, that singer. Or about wanting to meet everyone he's ever met again all over. That's it! Isn't it? How we met all those people, and how many of them stayed with us? How many of those people we met are with you right now? I get the rag and with my shirt off I feel like my brother Carl. I feel like Carl with my shirt off and my fat belly newly fat and my chest covered in a pattern of chest hair that looks like an Eagle with its head to the side and outstretched wings. We are in the neighborhood now. That ranch, where I used to live, that place I treated like a shithole. There were never any chores there. But this neighborhood, this cul-de-sac, it comes ready-made to rent with chores. We are wash-rag in hand. Starting to wash the wet truck. The world isn't good enough for you. But we always start washing the hood first, don't we? The windshield next. Then the roof of the cab. Here's the thing. You're not supposed to get water into the inside of the truck. Not of your brother's truck. Not when he's not here anymore. The thing is you are supposed to show that there's something to this! This isn't lying around under a palm tree with your shirt off and some young person to rub lotion on her or you. The thing to this is to show you care about this thing that is your brother's, now that he's not here anymore under this sky. If I can get in there and really get this clean, I can show him something somehow about how I feel about my brother. Oh, no I haven't told you that the postcard had a palm tree on it that that editor sent me. I cared enough to keep the truck. I sold my own car. I owe money on this grey Ford that is Carl's. Who wishes I could hug him around one more time and say I won't go on that stupid adventure? Maybe I wish I could undo that peyote ceremony that took me off the planet but I'm still on the planet. What I have to do is get these little balls of tar off. I wouldn't let the bank take the truck back. It's not new. It's a Ford. It's in good shape. I turn the hose from the spigot back on and rinse the hood and roof and the rest of the truck I get wet. I soak the dishtowel again in the soapy water and pull it out and start working on the bumper. It's pretty new. Carl put a brush guard on it and a cover on the back of hard diamond patterned spray-on-coating-over-metal and it's done right. Catherine is still with the Spaniard, Manuely. Jewely is running off and I keep calling her back, making a scene with no shirt on. The music is playing loudly. My mother, I speak to. My father is still so young looking. I have a job teaching freshman English. My pancreas is fine. I don't drink. At the bar I drink tonic water. I smoke cigs. I drink coffee. AA. I shout in English class. I see women. I mow the yard. I do chores. I go to Wyoming and ride horses with the boys in Bondurant. I'm going against my instincts. As a kid I always wanted whatever chore my brother chose first on Saturday morning at the wooden table eating eggs with mother and Dad. She got remarried this summer and my brother with the biggest heart in the world went to the wedding [two years ago plus] because I said I was going and my sister said she was going.

The wedding was in Hawaii and we were the last ones to show up, as per her travel arrangements made for us. Our mother was fake crying speaking to all her friends when we got there. My brother smuggled some pot and he and our sister had been drinking since we landed and we were waiting to get on the ferry. He was taking bong hits out of a little plastic bomb looking device on the ferry outside up on the top of the ferry above the water, which has dolphins under the surface and fish and sharks and whales. Oh, my mother was wearing a silver grey cloth around her and standing on the luau grounds and fake crying with her hand on her heart. I forgive her and want her to find happiness. Maybe she has. My brother, all of him, so big and with such true brown eyes, Carl, he showed up and we were all standing there and she wouldn't even acknowledge his presence. I wish you could see him. Know him. Maybe you do. And if not, this is just a goddamn book. It's not everything. Find God. Find love, Find America. The oldest child, the son, and she wouldn't even notice he was there. The wedding was a quarter million dollars and she never acknowledged he was there and she was going to get all the money and keep it and there was my brother like a boy who rode his motorcycle all over the earth and carried his heart with him and always had a beer and a hug for anyone and would throw his arms up in the air and mean it at any rock-and-roll concert worth being at, like he was on a roller coaster, and who would do anything for anyone, and there she was marrying this Jewish doctor (and if we know one thing from Christ's story, it's fuck doctors, any-how! Jew or not Jew. This isn't about Jews. I'm saying eat shit, Doctors. Except my cousin. Wink to you.) she cheated with, even after the chores and seeing her naked and being a kid and being her and being Dad and being boys, and she couldn't care less she was trying to find her happiness and having a tenth of a million dollar wedding in Hawaii. I know I said a quarter mil and then said a tenth of a mil. Sue me. And of course she cares. It was half a million dollars! It's all a wreck and it is what it is. Well, I can't tell you what that did to him, but he isn't here anymore and the truck is and I'm scratching the balls of tar through the cloth going against my instincts and really trying to do something one hundred percent for once. Really, I'm trying to get every little star of tar off the truck. I was all around the truck at the plastic parts at the black little dots that remind me of stars and of decay and I think of my brother and I try to clean everything for him to show him I care so much for him in a way I never showed him when he was here because I always half-assed everything which is why my name isn't in lights. I was always the one to half-ass everything and skip off and was a screw-off and he was the one who did things right and learned them all until he had them down by heart. I call the dog again. A car drives by with a girl. My shirt is off. She drives by. I keep to the chores.

If I can get each dot off I will do this right. I'm getting each dot. If I can get in there and get each dot off, then I am not skipping up and screwing-off like I always do. I'm getting tired and a little crabby in my forearm. I call the dog. Jewely. I call her. The car is long gone with the girl in it. I call the dog. I get her to come back. I turn the hose on and rinse off the plastic parts of the truck and get the whole truck wet again. I listen to the music. The man is singing the same things he was singing before. You don't deserve this. Really, you deserve silver lamps, oysters, cocktails, and cigarettes in a room at the Plaza Hotel. A big one! Your name in lights. Another highway to ride. The next big thing. Adventure. Here is music. There is no end. You don't even die when you die. There are girls and boys. There is so much truck to wash. Baby, when it's gone it is gone. Or is it? There are chores. So many little balls of tar to clean and show how much you care, bent over, humping it out in the sun. You give it your all. You keep going. You have more and more power to handle it all. You get the post card and it doesn't mean anything. You dunk the washcloth into the bucket and pull the soaped towel into the day and you keep at it. You got to show someone who isn't here anymore that you love him...you have got to show the whole world you have what it takes to love them. You have done chores. I've done peyote. I've been crazy since bananas. You know that you are inside yourself with all that has happened and all you have seen and you have got to get a move on anyhow. There are palm trees out there. There is the whole wide world of the past. It's noonday—and there's a whole lot more to come. Here's the last story: Books are over. Don't read a book, don't read any book. Don't read this book.